THE EIGHTH DAY
OF THE WEEK

THE EIGHTH DAY
OF THE WEEK

ALFRED R. KESSLER

Design & Composition by Shannon Gentry
Cover Photograph by Susan Kaufman

"Foreign Affairs". Copyright © 1958 by Stanley Kunitz, from
The Poems of Stanley Kunitz 1928-1978 by Stanley Kunitz.
Used by permission of W.W. Norton & Company, Inc.

Library of Congress Catalog Card Number: 00-101771
Kessler, Alfred
The Eighth Day of the Week / Alfred Kessler
ISBN: 1-929355-00-9

Published by Pleasure Boat Studio
8630 Wardwell Road
Bainbridge Island ·WA 98110-1589 USA
Tel/Fax: 1-888-810-5308
E-mail: pleasboat@aol.com
URL: http://www.pbstudio.com

First Printing

To Charlotte,
without whom time would not exist.

...
Tempers could sharpen knives, and do: we live
In states provocative
Where frowning headlines scare the coffee cream
And doomsday is the eighth day of the week.

From "Foreign Affairs" by Stanley Kunitz

MONDAY

'Don't look at everything,' my father said. His arm was around my waist as we turned in everlasting circles. He had taken me for my first merry-go-round ride, standing beside me as the horse with the wooden head and the smiling mouth went up and down, heedless of its rider. I was frightened. The world was going in one direction and I in the other. I grabbed the horse's neck and closed my eyes.

'Now, open your eyes. Slowly. And look at only one thing at a time.' My father's voice was deep and his speech unhurried as if every word was important. 'Look at something that's standing still, something that's going in the same direction as you are.

Look at the girl's head in front of you, the little blond girl who's sitting on the rabbit. Concentrate on her head and you won't feel dizzy.'

Seeing her in her usual place, I look past her into the mirror behind the bar as I do each evening, trying to postpone the meaning of her face, allowing her mouth, her nose, the depths of her blue eyes to grow on me gradually, to give me courage, to erase memories I do not want.

The mirror, yellow with age but spotlessly clean, reflects the familiar signs of the storefronts across the street, their inverted lettering confusing me as much today as it did when I was a young man. Only the mysterious scrawls in Arabic that have always seemed directionless to me calm my mind.

The street outside is quiet now. It's too late for traffic, too late for the lingering strains of Levantine music to drift from the stores as effortlessly as the exotic odors from within and, at this time of year when the evenings are hot from the setting sun, it's too early for the weight of night and the glare of street lights to oppress me. Only those like ourselves are about—the diversion of a restaurant, the comfort of a bar. Others who have lives to lead are already home.

She has crossed her legs and is seated comfortably on the high stool. As is becoming for her age, she pulls her skirt to her knees covering the still sharply outlined prominences of her smooth bones. Then she touches her glass to her lips.

That's my signal, the touching of the glass to her lips, the sign that tells me it's the moment to approach her. I pick up my martini. My glass is already half empty. My hand shakes just a little. The green olive sits in its depression above the stem as if captured by its own weight like a bottom-scrounging fish rocking imperceptibly with the gentle movements of the depths.

By necessity I nurse my martinis. I also have memories of martinis that I wish to avoid. My limit now is three per evening. And always with the same olive. The salt I used to love has also been limited by the medical dictates of everlasting life.

I'm standing next to her. In the mirror our eyes meet for a moment then hers drift back to her drink searching for the response she knows she will give.

"You have a very fine face for a woman leaning on a bar." Turning to her, I smile, the smile that others used to call charming. "Or should I say that I can see that at one time it was a fine face."

"Thanks a lot." She doesn't look at me but, as she touches her lips once more to the edge of the glass, I see the lines in her skin through her makeup. The web of crisscrosses are more obvious when her face is still than when she moves, pursing her lips, drinking, talking, doing something purposeful.

"More than fine," I say, motioning with my hand in her direction. "Intelligent."

I long to touch her face, to take her chin between my failing fingers and turn her head to me. But I'm afraid. As with the martinis and the salt, we too have set our limits. She must accept my stare and see my desires on her own.

She must want them.

"Or is *fine* a better word than *intelligent*? A face with breeding behind it."

She laughs, the controlled calm notes of one who is amused. Still she doesn't look at me.

"May I sit with you?" I ask.

"The stool is empty. Hardly anyone here. It's a quiet night."

"Perhaps it's too early.

"It's never too early."

"I thought the saying was, 'It's never too late.'"

Finally, she turns her head showing a hint of melancholy in her eyes. "You sound like a priest. I don't like preaching."

"I'm not preaching. Just talking."

The stem of the glass that I hold between my fingers is as smooth as her arm resting on the bar. Her summer dress ends above her elbows. But the cloth is sheer and I can see the curve of her shoulders and the white straps of her brassiere pressing lightly into her flesh. Unlike the fine wrinkles in her face, her throat and chest still match the freshness in her eyes.

As I tilt the glass to my mouth, the olive strikes my lips reminding me of the cool kiss of a child rushing off to school or of a son being told by his mother what to do: 'Now kiss your father. And say goodnight. That's a good boy.'

And that's my second signal of the evening, the olive striking my lips, a signal not of anticipation but of an empty glass. I know. I know. I drank too fast. It is sometimes a habit of mine, especially when I'm nervous or somewhat disturbed.

Remember, I'm supposed to nurse martinis. And now all I have left is the olive touching my lips. How I long to part them and taste the olive, to feel the soft red pimento with my tongue.

"Another, Doctor?"

"Please, Tom." I have known the bartender since he was a child. Once when he was young I saved his life. Or so his parents thought. This was his father's bar when I was a student long before he was born. Instead of martinis then, it was beer—but only on weekends.

"And save the olive. Right, Doctor?"

"Right, Tom."

He smiles at her sitting next to me. "And Missus? Not quite ready? I'll be back."

When I was a student at the College of Medicine a few blocks away, booths lined the walls of this bar. On Friday and Saturday nights, after studying or after our duties at the hospital were over, some of us would gather in the booths to lighten the efforts of our week, some of us alone and others with girls. Excluded from our tame weekend revelries, not because of choice but because of their inaccessibility, were the young ladies from the Heights, the quiet neighborhood of proud old houses that stretches along the river from the road I see in the mirror to the Brooklyn Bridge.

Now tables have replaced the booths. The room seems more modern, or should I say, more fashionable. And, by the same token, light has replaced the shadows, transforming hidden corners into open space. But through all the newfound brilliance, the bar is the same old bar, the long yellow-tinted mirror is the same, even the overhead fans are the same. The substance of the old has been arranged discreetly and not merely left to rot with age.

Personally, I preferred the comfort of the booths to the advantages of the tables. Now, you can choose to sit alone at a small table or gather as many chairs as you wish around a larger one. With only a glass in your hand and a few words in your mouth, crowding is never a problem in this bar for, you see, food has never been served here. This is a drinking bar with only peanuts, potato chips and the like. If at times it becomes necessary, the bartender can make coffee. Good coffee too. But food? No. Not even a sandwich. The street abounds with Lebanese and Syrian restaurants, so why should a bar try to compete?

Ah! Talk of competition. My other evening companion has finally arrived, making my life more complete and my designs more certain. She is always half an hour later than I, but tonight I missed her grand entrance. My thoughts were wandering in the booths that had lined the dark walls of years ago.

Yet, facing the mirror as I do each evening and thus having advantage of the entire room, I know her practiced ways by heart. The deliberate manner in which she opens the door then steps across the threshold merely to hesitate hides the timid nature shown by her downcast eyes. Once in the light, she closes the door, raises her eyelids and looks around, perhaps still longing for the attention that was once so easily procured.

What is she up to now? She's stopped halfway to her accustomed table and is nodding to people, smiling her hesitant smile. She never does a thing like that even though most of the customers in the bar know her or have heard about her past.

Perhaps she thinks I'm neglecting her for the woman next to me and is giving me a second chance.

God! And there she goes again looking straight at me. Is that a frown of disappointment on her face? I'm sorry, my dear. I have disappointed others also.

With a certain stateliness and a suggestive sway to her hips, she continues the full length of the room. Some young fellows at the other end of the bar are smiling at her, mocking her movements with their heads. What do they know, poor innocent fools?

She has reached her table near the far corner and arranges

her chair to face me. Do others save that table for her? To-night, there's hardly a soul in the bar, but even on busy nights the small table with one chair remains free until she arrives.

Something is different about her tonight, some small de-tail that distorts her natural look of an aging beauty. Her hair. Yes. That's it, her hair. She's been to the beauty parlor again. Her hair is too yellow, too stiff, too formally done. Yet looking at her, I cannot deny her attractiveness. Not as attractive as the quiet woman beside me, the one who sips her drink and avoids my eyes as if she fears them and whose hand I would love to touch. I turn and steal a glance at her, at her straight posture on the barstool, at the firm curve of her thigh.

And then I look back at the other woman who is adjust-ing the neckline of her dress. Not bad either. But not as much class. Yet I must admit that older women maintain their bod-ies better today than when I was young. I remember my mother. She wasn't fat but was what she called stout. Nowadays, if they're wearing clothes, they all look good, at least to me.

"I thought you came to talk."

I turn to her. She's looking straight into the mirror, tip-ping her head back, draining the last drop from her glass, show-ing her white neck, tilting her breasts slightly upward.

"I'm sorry. Sometimes my mind wanders."

No. I haven't forgotten her sitting next to me. If she had looked at me a moment ago she would have discovered my covetous glance. She's so close I can feel her warmth melting the artificial air that covers us. Her humidity crawls over my skin on this hot July night, sticking to me like sheets in an exhausted bed. I would like to stare at her as intensely as I do at the table far across the room. If, at this close distance, I stared at the still beautiful creature beside me with the wildness I know is in my eyes, would she think me mad? Would my eyes betray me as they once had?

Would my tongue shift the blame to her?

"You might at least beckon to Tom. My glass is empty."

And so is mine. Completely empty. All I have left is my olive. At least I'm cautious with that.

I signal to Tom. He's an alert young man. Like his father was. His father used to give us advice years ago. Imagine, a bartender giving advice to medical students. 'That kid's got her eye on you,' he had told me. 'You'd better play up to her old man. He's important. But don't let him know you bring her here.'

How I wish Tom's father were still alive. He was so easy to talk to. And so wise. I'm sure Tom is the same way. But the age difference between us inhibits me.

Tom arrives with a bottle of Glenfiddich, the brand of scotch my companion always drinks. He pours it in her glass. From marveling at his steady hand my gaze shifts to her. For a change she's looking at me and I can almost feel her golden hair against my face, hair more true in color than the woman's at the table, loose instead of stiff, weightless. Surely, she must visit a different hairdresser, an artist, one who knows what she is like.

Tom looks at my empty glass and his eyebrows rise. They're bushy like his father's were and match his curly hair. "You empty too, Doctor? Sure you want another so soon?"

"It will be my third and my last."

He takes my glass and I glance at the woman beside me. The fine creases in her face have deepened and her blue eyes seem cold behind her high cheekbones. She's frowning at me in the mirror, her lips compressed into a silent line. I feel ashamed but cannot keep my eyes from her. She looks as beautiful annoyed as when she's calm.

"What's your hurry tonight?" she finally asks. "Worried about your lady friend in the corner? Every night you sit with me and stare at her. You must know the lady pretty well. What's your interest in her? Even from here I can see the longing in her eyes. She would love to be with you. Tell me, who is she?"

"My wife."

This time, when the olive touches my lips, I open them and let the olive slip into the cavity of my mouth. Before biting through the smooth skin, my tongue brushes the fruit from one side of my mouth to the other, twirling it like my merry-go-round of childhood, letting it skim past my teeth, holding it against my cheek, feeling its perfect shape, finally squeezing it slowly, gently against my palate until the thin thread of pimento extrudes itself. And then, suddenly, I crush it with my teeth and swallow fast...because it's tasteless. The gin has robbed it of the salt I love.

My third martini. Finished. Too bad.

But I know my Tom. I must go. Just one final look across the room. She sits alone at her small table as always, waiting for what never comes, looking furtively in different directions and then staring at me as if I might respond. If I could help, my dear, I would. But my days of helping are over.

And now one last sly glance to my side. I have become quite adept at sly glances, even avoiding my own eyes in the mirror as I shave.

She doesn't see me examining her. At least I hope not. The evening has worn away some of her makeup. The lines around her eyes and around her mouth, especially those on her upper lip, are more obvious than they were. But it makes little difference because through her dress her body is perfect. At least her undergarments make it appear that way.

"Thank you for talking to me," I say.

"It was my pleasure." Her eyes look sad. "You are all right?"

"As well as I will ever be."

The bar is still all but empty, occupied only by habitués like me and my two nightly companions. Thank God the medical school moved from the neighborhood years ago. I wonder what the students would have thought if they had seen their professor drinking here every night. Or what her father would have thought. Her father would never have been seen here. Or anywhere else like it. He wasn't a snob. But he knew where he belonged. He was a gentleman and the finest teacher I ever had.

Oh well, I won't have to think or worry about my reputation much longer.

Half circling the room, I walk the long way from my one companion at the bar to my other companion at her table. I must look ridiculous doing this every night. Everyone in the bar knows. They know her as well as they know me. But I feel that it's my duty to do what I'm doing. All my training has focused on duty. Responsibility and duty. But that was a long time ago. Anyway...duty or not, I believe that I'm giving her a little thrill. And thrills are hard to come by at our age.

I nod at her. I try not to smile. I must do nothing encouraging. Just something to show my civility. She always looks up at me with an anxious longing in her eyes as though I might say something, suggest something. Don't worry, my dear. I won't.

As I head towards the door, I look at my friend still sitting at the bar. She's shaking her head from side to side. Her mouth opens. It must be a sigh escaping from her perfect lips, a warm breath that I would love to have heard or, better, to have felt.

I pause before the door, wave to Tom but avoid that last glance at my two companions. So, once more, it's good night again.

The heat outside hits me like a fist after the comfort of the bar. The sky is dark but not too dark. A trace of light hangs over Manhattan and the Upper Bay and in the heavy air I smell the sea.

The streets are empty on this Monday night and the Lebanese and Syrian restaurants have hardly any customers. Weekends exhaust people...or is it simply the apprehension of renewing another seven days?

Before turning down my tree-lined street, I walk past my two favorite restaurants just to smell the smells that I have known for so long. At the corner I stop and look behind me. Nothing yet, but it won't be long. There. See it? The glow from her golden hair beneath the street lamp. Every night she leaves the bar shortly after me and walks along the same path as I. Of course I know where she lives. Less than half a block away. But I cannot visit her. She will only see me in public.

I walk up the steps to my house and stand before the beautifully sculptured front door, a double door painted an imposing black. The brass door handles and the foot plates shine in the dark. I fumble with my keys not because of the three martinis or of my trembling hands but because I want to hear her footsteps as she passes, hear her heels striking stone, playing a rhythm I know so well until the sound of her is gone.

It takes so short a time to lose sounds and sights...and

the happiness that once was yours.

The lights in the hall are easy to find. The grand staircase leading to my bedroom is covered with heavy carpet insuring a devouring silence. I hear myself sigh, once and then twice, confirming my own solitude. My mouth? Am I breathing through my mouth? Yes. I touch my lips and feel the warm flow of air against my fingertips.

An open mouth. Just right for a little drink. But no more martinis. I have had my limit. And I keep my word. I learned that from her father too…to keep my word. But whiskey is nice at bedtime. It doesn't show as much.

Oh, God! This big house!

TUESDAY

This evening I'm late…something unusual for me.

Being late now and then is understandable, or at least excusable, especially considering the unforeseen turn my life has taken and the way I've changed. Oh, I've changed. I know it. I don't deny it. Still, I've tried to maintain certain traits, characteristics, high points I was noted for. And one of them is promptness. I'm always on time…even now that time has become my nemesis.

Today I was detained against my will. Yet I held my impatience and my boredom to myself. I was polite, another quality I've retained.

'Always be polite, Peter,' my mother said. 'It'll get you more than all those fine grades on your report card that your father is so proud of.'

But these staff conferences, these late afternoon talk marathons, are beginning to wear me out. I ask myself why should I be polite any longer? Why try?

As I open the door to the bar, the cool air clears my head of the day's annoyances.

For a Tuesday evening in July the bar is rather full.

No cloud of smoke blinds my eyes as in my student days but the din of lonely voices trying to communicate reminds me of my childhood and the tangled murmur of prayers in a crowded church.

But I find them easily. My two blondes. Or should I say my two companions, my two lady friends. They're in their habitual places, one at the bar and the other at her table.

This evening each of them arrived before me. As I entered, I caught both of them looking at the door but the lady at the bar turned quickly, trying to pretend that her glance was casual. The one at the table is more curious by nature and is now following my steps across the room. I give her a slight bow and move my lips. Perhaps she thinks it's a sign of a whispered word, whispered in her ear at night. Or perhaps a kiss, seen by no one but felt by two.

I head towards my companion at the bar. Not only is her back turned to me but she's looking elsewhere in the mirror. As far as timing is concerned, I don't exist as yet. As I've said, she has more class.

"Pardon me," I say. A big fellow with shoulders padded with the flesh of a football player is crowding the bar next to my companion talking to someone about the same size as he. "May I get a little closer so that I can order. Thank you."

Not a very pleasant nod from him. Not the type of response my mother would have taught me.

'Smile,' *my mother said. 'Even if you don't mean it.'*

Now that he has moved his bulk, I'm at last where I should be, where I want to be, next to my companion who has the good manners and the forbearance to let me spend my evenings talking to her.

But before I recognize her presence, before I say one word, my eyes must drift to the mirror. I want to see her slowly, let her grow on me. I want to form an impression of what I already know she is, just to prolong that moment of exaltation I've been waiting for.

She too has turned to face the mirror and is looking straight ahead, not at me but as if her mind were occupied by the street outside, studying a scene she has known all her life, lost in the uncertainty of her own knowledge.

Ah! That sudden flash of blue. I caught her eye. In all the time I've known her, I've never failed to catch her eye no matter what has happened.

But it is I who turn away, not because of the intimacy of our momentary contact but because of the mirror. Now that I have formed my impression, the mirror has become an obstacle and I want to see her as she is. I want to see her skin and her body and the clothes that she is wearing as they are and not as they appear through a flat, cold surface.

Whenever I turn my head, for an instant I always think that I'm on my merry-go-round. The world is flashing by somewhere far beyond me. The objects that surround me and all the thoughts that crowd my head become a blur, relieving me from acknowledging them or understanding them or having to be part of them. Details are wiped away as if by someone else, by fate, by circumstances. What happens is no longer my responsibility. My conscience is clean. When I was a kid I loved merry-go-rounds.

Finally…she lifts her glass. It's been resting on the bar far too long, her long fingers relaxed on its rounded surface. Now she purses her lips, an unnecessary movement to the function of drinking but one that adds a mystery, a sensuousness to her behavior.

And that's my signal. I wait until her lips have parted from the glass as if something were slipping from them. A faint hint of red remains on the transparent surface. Can an inanimate object be lucky?

"You have a very fine face for a woman leaning on a bar." I smile my usual smile.

"Or should I say that I can see that at one time it was a fine face." Now when did we decide upon that line? Her face still is a fine face. My mother would never have approved of my gentle dig. And neither do I. It's inappropriate.

"Thanks a lot." What is she doing? She keeps looking at me when she should turn away. And a gleam lights her eye. "But you always have a martini in your hand when you say that."

"Forgive me. I'm late."

"Not an emergency case, like when you were young?"

"There are no emergencies any longer. Just trivialities I must still put up with."

I signal to Tom. He always comes to me no matter how

busy he is. He has fidelity.

He has never forgotten what he considers an obligation. His father taught him manners as my mother taught me. But his father taught him other things as well.

"Good evening, Doctor. Hope you've had a good day."

"Fine, Tom."

"The usual?"

"Please."

Her eyes have finally turned from me to the mirror as they're supposed to, leaving me gaping like a love-sick youth at her hair, her profile, remembering the lost gleam in her eye. So, for appearances' sake, I'm forced to turn my head away as she has done and gaze again into the mirror to hide my lustful desires from those around me. Yet, if the truth be known, I can really see more of her in the mirror, not just her profile but the full beauty of her face.

Do mirrors tells us more than we want to know if we look carefully? Because there at the far end of the room I see my other companion at her table. She's running her fingers along the tabletop, tapping them as rapidly as a horse galloping from here to nowhere.

"Your friend back there has been very nervous tonight waiting for you." Her voice tells me that she's facing me again. I don't have to look because her eyes are like fire on my skin.

"It doesn't hurt her," I say.

"How do you know?"

"Because she's been waiting for a long time. Even longer than I. Waiting was part of her profession. So she should be used to it."

"There are things some of us can never grow used to."

I shrug my shoulders and sigh. "We can only try."

For an instant our eyes meet, binding us as firmly as the pain of secrets. Like forms seen from a merry-go-round, other objects in the room merge into nothing and, if only for a moment, we two know each other's mute souls.

It's strange how often eyes meet, those of parents, lovers, children, total strangers, and we feel what they feel but do nothing about it. We look away and abandon them.

My friend at the table does seem nervous tonight, something more than her usual self-consciousness. Her fingers have finally calmed and are reaching for her glass. Her glass is shaking. She brings her other hand to hold it between her palms then cautiously lifts it to her lips as if praying some hopeless prayer.

"You've been looking at her for a long time. You must be worried too."

"I agree with you. She does look upset."

"Because you were late. And she was worried. Tell me. Who is she?"

"…My wife."

"Wives always worry—whether they're in love or not. But more so when they are in love. Why don't you walk past her?"

"I do that when I leave—after I've had my three martinis. And this martini is my first."

"Make believe you're going to the rest room. Go on. Have some pity. Like doctors are supposed to."

'Be kind to dumb animals,' my mother said. 'They never fight back unless you harm them.'

"Yes," I sigh. "You're right. Sometimes I forget myself. Forgive me."

I get up and finish my drink standing. The olive touches my lips. How I crave it, how I long for it to taste the way it should, the way I remember it when I was young...before it was diluted by time.

"Ask Tom to bring me another while I'm gone, will you please. And don't let this bulk of muscle standing next to me take my seat."

"Don't worry, I'm too old for him." She's actually smiling at me. I see her teeth, as white as a young girl's. Her tongue touches them. "And save the olive, right?"

"Right."

I prefer walking across rooms when they're crowded with people standing in groups, elbowing my way through them. But tonight most of the customers are sitting at tables or at the bar and it's too easy for me to find my way. When a room is crowded I bump into others or they bump into me, not purposefully but by accident, affording me the luxury of physical contact with other human beings that's not professional, a contact which I'm sorely lacking.

Professionally, whether a patient merely has some unimportant ailment or is facing impending death, her body is cold, an object to be examined and diagnosed, simply a thing, a fragment to be looked upon dispassionately. But touching the skin of someone you want or fantasize about or have never even seen before creates an exchange of human warmth, a comfort that lingers in your mind. You are real and so is she.

As I draw close to her table she looks up at me, her eyes as blue as her forlorn face. Why has she always looked frightened when I'm near her? She should know me well enough. Has she really felt that way for all these years? I'd thought it part of her approach, the gentle overture to a skilled performance.

Her fingers fumble with her glass. She pushes the glass along the wooden table top forgetting the coaster next to her, then folds her empty fingers together like a child in school while her gaze shifts from her hands to me as if expressing a timid invitation to join her.

I should speak to her but have no desire to. How far can pity go? Like everything else it has its limits. It wears out too. But why should I have pity? Who or what chooses the road we travel? If I had true pity—or should I say *charity?*—I would draw up a chair from another table and sit next to her. But what would I say? I know her now only from a distance.

I pause and as someone squeezes past me my thigh touches the edge of her table. Her glass trembles and she reaches for it. In apology I smile in a manner my mother would have approved of, not in greeting but in acknowledgment.

To make my misguided adventure seem plausible to others and even to myself, I go to the rest room, wash my hands as is my frequent habit, and look at my face in the mirror. Living alone for all these years has aged me before my time. Except for my full head of black hair, grayed only at the temples, I look older than I really am. Perhaps it's the silence I endure at night that has weighed upon my face and mind.

No one else is in the rest room. The door is closed and the handle is still. Quickly, once then twice, I turn and spin around, not enough to make me dizzy but enough to feel that I'm on my merry-go-round again.

'**P**oppa! Pop! Take me to the carnival! Take me to Coney Island! I want to ride the merry-go-round. Wasn't my report card the best I've ever had?'

When I grew older than the little boy I'd been and my arms grew long enough, my father taught me how to lean sideways in the imitation saddle and reach far out to collect the rings, the one attraction that lured young men from more thrilling rides to display their skill and gain admiring looks from their young ladies.

'You must aim for more than one ring,' my father said. 'Each time around, you must get at least two. But always try for three. The more you get, the more chance you'll have for the golden ring. Never accept anything that isn't perfect because when you're a doctor everything you do will have to be perfect.'

I stop turning myself in the merry-go-round of my mind and look at my hands while they're still glistening with water. They have tried to reach for perfection.and some might think they've attained it. But I laugh at them, both at my admirers and my hands, especially my hands. The skin is as smooth and as white as a woman's.

I have washed them often enough.

As I pass the lonely creature I've just forsaken, I ignore her. Instead I look at all the busy heads enjoying themselves. More people are crowding at the bar than when I had left but my companion has her purse on my stool and my drink in front of it, clear and without ice, mixed by Tom as it should be mixed and not simply on the rocks. Tom knows I dislike a toothpick in the olive.

"Did you cheer her up?"

"You look at her and tell me if she's more or less nervous than she was. I was too close to notice."

"Did you say something to her? Something soothing?"

"No."

"Do you ever say anything to her?"

"No."

"You talk to me."

"That's different. I want to talk to you. You're the only one I have left to talk to."

"How can you say that? A man who's busy all day with his staff and his students."

"Look into my eyes. Please." I almost reach for her.

"I know your eyes too well."

"Of course you do." I turn my head away.

Silence is more bearable when disguised by noise. The large young man next to me laughs with all his weight at each joke he tells and his friend laughs back. From the distance, someone is calling for Tom and at the furthest end of the room behind my lady friend's table, a young girl, surrounded by three young men, begins to sing. Her voice is deep and clear.

Through the mirror, both my companion and I are looking at the young girl.

We cannot help but see my lady friend sitting at her table.

"I think she's less nervous than she was. See her tapping her hand in rhythm to the girl's song instead of searching for you?"

"Diversions help," I say.

We turn from the mirror and face each other. Her eyes are laughing. How nice to see. But she tries to conceal her amusement with a frown.

"For instance," I say, "I'm enjoying a diversion at this very moment."

"And what's that?"

I glance into her lap. "Your knees. Do you know they're showing? I rarely see them. Tell me why you're so careful not to show your knees. It's the fashion today to show much more than that. And your knees are still lovely."

"It's my age."

I see the playfulness in her eyes again as she adjusts her hem. She leans towards me. "Or perhaps it's your age to think they're still lovely."

"Come now. Be objective."

"Objective? Impossible. You must know that I can only feel." Her smile looks worn. "You see, I haven't changed."

"Do you think you could try?"

"I would really like to. If I could only forget."

"Please try. For me."

She pauses and looks away. Then she turns and faces me directly. "Only if we stop talking trivia as we do each night and you tell me a story," she says.

"What story?"

She is quiet for a minute. Finally her lips begin to move, slowly as if she is thinking to herself and her face remains without expression. "Your story. And the story of the woman who is your wife. Just tell the truth."

"I'm afraid that you know it."

"I would like to hear it from you."

I wave to Tom. He looks at me as his father would have...or my father would have, two wise uneducated men who knew about life.

'What's your job, Pop?' I asked. 'Johnnie's father sells insurance.'

'Look at my hands, Pete. Now hold yours up to mine. See the difference. Mine are bricklayer's hands.'

'Now wash those hands before you sit down to eat,' my mother said to him before each meal. But I loved my father's hands and the feel of his rough skin on mine, skin as rough as the sidewalk outside our house. Whenever we walked together I took his hand in mine.

We lived three blocks from the river in a rented flat on the second floor of a two-family house.

'Don't you dare go near that awful river,' my mother said. 'Stay where I can find you.'

And if she hadn't seen me for half an hour, her stout figure, clad in the apron she always wore, would be leaning out the window.

'Peter! Peter, where are you? It's time for your glass of milk.'

The kitchen window of our apartment looked out onto a small backyard that had been crowded into a patch of damp dirt by a two-car garage. When I was by myself with nothing to do, I sat at this rear window rather than at the windows facing the street where the view was blocked by an overgrown poplar tree.

At the rear window I could see over the flat roofs of our neighbors' houses and play games with what I saw. Looking past the garage at the clothes pole at the end of our yard, I would align it with the tower of the bridge that crossed my mother's evil river. Closing one eye, I'd move my head slowly in one direction while the clothes pole traveled along the length of the bridge seemingly by itself. Then, as I moved my head faster and faster until I was almost dizzy, my clothes pole became the lance of a mounted warrior charging over barricades and flying off to someplace else. Or, if my mother had hung her wash on the line to dry and become soft in the sun, I made believe that the swollen sheets were sails, propelling me and my ship along the forbidden river to another land.

Every evening my father stopped for a beer in the local bar before supper. My mother didn't approve but there was nothing she could do about it. For me the sound of his footsteps climbing the stairs meant that my evening with him was about to begin. He would enter the kitchen and hold my mother by the shoulders. She offered him her cheek as he kissed her then she would screw her face into a scowl as if the smell of beer had contaminated her.

While my mother finished the last-minute preparations for our supper, my father and I sat at the kitchen table talking, sometimes in tones so low that my mother would cry out, 'What did you say? What was that?' He always had something to tell me about his day: a funny incident on the subway, the design of the building he was working on, new people he had met. And after supper the three of us, the entire family, sat in the living room that was also my parents' bedroom and listened to the radio.

'You'll have a more interesting life than this,' my father would say, 'when you're a doctor.'

My mother would simply shake her head and sigh, perhaps brush something off my shirt, touch me with her fingers. 'You're filling his head with dreams again. Pure nonsense. Do you know how much your dreams would cost?'

"**Y**our story. I'm waiting."

Tom is an ideal bartender. His eye is all over the place. He observes more than most of my resident physicians at the hospital do, and more quickly too. He keeps his customers happy, amused and sober. He knows each and every one of them because, in fact, he's their silent confessor.

"How about another, Tom?"

"It'll be your third, Doctor."

"And my last, Tom."

Trying to avoid attention I bring my martini close to me. My index finger plunges into the shallow glass and I stir the olive, playing with it in its transparent cage as I played with the poor woman at the table, walking up to her, hesitating and showing my practiced look of concern without ever having

33

the slightest intention of saying a word. But she must have known what I was up to. She certainly must have grown used to my weaknesses even back then.

The olive? Now what would I do if some impulse forced me to put two fingers into the glass, snare the olive and hold it in my hand? Could I keep my action secret? Would I hide the olive tightly in my fist like a miser concealing his gold because it wasn't yet time to devour it? Remember, I wait for the olive. I want the olive. Like the woman at the table waiting in vain? Or perhaps myself...waiting and waiting...and waiting?

But look at her now in the depths of the mirror. She's sitting at her table completely absorbed by the girl who's singing. Could that be a smile on her face? I don't believe it. Yet her face is the type of face that should be smiling. She has a fine face. Or one that once was fine.

I close my eyes to the mirror, squeezing my lids as tightly as I can. That damned mirror can become my entire view of life and hide what I want to see, what I want to know, what I want to have. Because what I think I see in the mirror confuses me...like people I know, myself, the letters on the stores across the street. I can't believe that everything in the mirror is backwards. But it is. Except for the signs in Arabic that mean absolutely nothing to me.

But why close my eyes? What good does it do? Simply closing my eyes is a poor substitute for my merry-go-round because nothing spins when I close my eyes. No subjective sensation races through my blood and excites me. Only the darkness that my closed lids offer allows me to escape from myself...but for too short a time.

If I could stop this foolish thinking, if I could quiet my

restless brain, I might feel that I had died or at least been placed in a state of suspension. Peace? Calm? Suspended animation? Is that what I want? A state of unconsciousness? If I were unconscious, my mind and my tongue would be silent. Not even I would know. But then, hope as I might, something would undoubtedly force me to open my eyes again and immediately I would be aware of all that has happened.

But before I open them now I would like to have one last pleasure.

In the dark that I have produced I lick the taste of the martini off my finger then raise the glass to my lips.

"Drink it slowly," she whispers close to my ear.

She touched my wrist! I can't believe it. She touched my wrist. I felt her warm fingers against my skin. I know she touched my wrist. Why weren't my eyes open?

"I'm still waiting. Are you going to tell me your story as I asked. Or are you trying to forget it?"

I open my eyes and look at her, not at her face but at her body and her arms and her hands whose heat I have just felt.

Each night she wears a different dress and in summer I can see through the fine clothes she has the good taste to buy, through the covering of shaded cloth that allows her body to breathe. There's nothing suggestive about her dresses. If anything they're too conservative for my taste. But they let me imagine, they let me hope.

Tonight she's wearing a red dress, not brazen, almost pink, again with short sleeves covering her shoulders but with a wide neckline revealing the beautiful forms of her collar bones and the gentle hollows above. If only she had the boldness to show more of her chest. But at least the bodice of her dress is tight and I can see her ribs move with each breath she takes.

She's crossing her legs and her loose hem, like some errant breeze in the heat of a summer night, slides along her stockings exposing her knees and the fold of her thigh meeting her calf. No. This time I won't tell her what I've seen. I'll keep it to myself.

"I'm still waiting for your story while you contemplate your beloved olive."

I start to raise my glass again.

"No." she says. "Leave the glass on the bar. You still have a little left. Save it."

"It's late. Really, I should finish my drink and go. Remember, I must work in the morning."

"Are you going to tell me your story or not?"

"Yes. If you insist...I'll try."

"I want to hear it from you."

"Then for tonight, let me only begin. I must tell this story slowly, in installments. You see, I have feelings too."

As if prompted by some memory, we both turn from the mirror and look directly at the woman sitting alone at her table. One hand is on her forehead brushing away a few strands of hair. The color looks less gaudy in the crowded bar than it did last night. She wipes her eyes.

"Loneliness is the saddest feeling in the world," my companion says.

I face her and almost place my hand on her knee. "Only because when you're lonely, you're thinking of past happinesses."

She motions to the woman at the table. "Suppose you had never known happiness."

"Everyone has known happiness. Haven't you?"

"Yes. At one time more than my share. But how do you

know that the happiness you think you're experiencing is real?"

"Because it's so easy and so simple to feel. Happiness just happens. Suddenly it's there. It's never planned. It exists without a formula or without reason. It may be meaningless to others, even to the person who makes you happy by what she does or the things she gives. The trouble with happiness is that it's fragile. Anything can break it and it can disappear in a moment. Look at the young girl across the room sitting behind our friend. She was singing a short while ago and now she's laughing. Look at her tossing her head and letting her hair fly from her face. She's happy and she knows it. But what might she be like in a few years? Or even later tonight? Will she merely be another copy of our friend? Will all her happiness be sucked from her?"

"Please, don't start at the end of your story. I want to hear the beginning."

"Then turn around. No! Don't look in the mirror. I want to see you."

Looking into each other's eyes for any length of time is difficult for us. Her eyes are moist, but not from tears. Actually I see a smile in them, the blue irises as bright as if they had been watered by a pleasant memory. She looks down at my idle hands and keeps her head bent. I see only her forehead and her hair.

"Go on. Get started," she whispers.

"Well. The story began with her father. But we'll skip that part for a while. Because at the time I didn't know that he was her father.

"I was living a few blocks from the medical school, or where the school used to be.

"No, I wasn't living in the Heights but in the neighborhood next to the Heights south of the street that we see in the mirror, the street that is backwards in our view.

"I was very lucky. An old friend of my mother's ran a rooming house for sailors down by the wharves and she offered my mother a room for me free of charge.

"My mother was very skeptical about my wish to be a doctor. Now don't get me wrong. She was very kind to me. She thought only of my well-being. With my father dead I knew she skimped on things more than ever before, especially things for herself, just to give me an allowance to survive the week at school. If she had known that I saved a few of our precious pennies for beer on weekends she would have been sadly disappointed."

'You'll never finish this foolishness you've started,' my mother said. 'Wanting to become a doctor. We don't belong to that class. If only you hadn't taken those wild dreams of your father to heart.'

"My mother knew where she belonged. She had no airs about her and no wish to go above her station. Her manners were perfect, perhaps a little affected at times, but always correct. Her mother had been a maid for a rich family in Manhattan and my mother was proud of that fact.

"Every Sunday, after a long week of study, I visited my mother for a few hours. After our noonday meal she would kiss me good-bye, wipe her eyes with her handkerchief and hand me my weekly allowance, 'Now you must eat well during the rest of the week...but try to manage frugally.'"

I look at my hands, my white, soft hands, and I think of my father's honest ones and his untimely death.

"My father's insurance sent me to school after the scaffolding on which he was working collapsed and fell to the ground."

I laugh, not with humor but at the insensitivity of fate, the constant sacrifice of one for another...perhaps the better for the lesser.

"My father filled me with the idea of perfection while he had the good fortune to live with simple human failings."

She's looking into my eyes again as if pleading with me to get to the happy part. But I love her eyes and must take them as they are. So seldom do they look at me with emotion that even sorrow revives my hopes.

"When I had time I would walk in the evenings to clear my head of studies and the bawdiness of sailors' talk. I learned a lot of sailors' talk in the rooming house. They were very frank in front of me. Perhaps they recognized me as really one of their own."

I begin laughing again, a different type of laughter, and touch my lips with my hand. "You know, I could stop this story, forget my manners and, if I wanted, shock you with all that I learned."

"Have you ever?"

"Never with my talk."

I pause again. She's biting her lower lip, showing her teeth, inflicting a minor pain.

"I always walked in the Heights. It was my idea of luxury...perfection, although I'd been told that the neighborhood had deteriorated compared to what it had been.

"One spring Saturday night, a night as warm as summer, a night like tonight, I met her. I was sitting on the ground along the bluff near the Penny Bridge watching the sun set beyond Manhattan. As if a fire were blazing behind them, the darkening silhouettes of the buildings reminded me of giant church steeples hovering over the boats in the river below, boats that seemed as small as Christmas toys.

"Suddenly two bare legs stopped in front of me blocking my view. From a pair of battered saddle shoes I saw two shapeless stems with threads of golden hair reflecting the final light of day. She had not yet begun to shave her legs.

"'What are you doing sitting there?' she asked me. She had the knees of a young girl, like those of a cherub, sexless. But before I knew it she squatted down in front of me, her face level with mine and smiled. 'Give me your hands.'

"For some reason I obeyed her and she pulled me to my feet in one strong tug.

"I fell forward and gained my balance only by grabbing her shoulders. 'I'm sorry,' I told her. I backed away. It was only then that I noticed her hair, combed back and held somewhere behind her head.

"'You're a danger to pedestrians,' she said. 'I almost tripped over you. Don't you know that in this snooty neighborhood you probably need a license to sit on the ground.'

"'You live here?'

"'Sure. But now only on weekends when I'm home from college.'

"'You're in college?'

"'Oh, I'm only a freshman. At Manhattanville. As far as I'm concerned, it's a waste of time living there during the week. It's simpler and more fun to take the subway. But my parents thought it would be good for me to associate with young ladies all day long. They say they've tried hard but their efforts worked only with my older sister.'

"She came closer and looked at me as though I were a

specimen in the lab. 'And you? Do you live here too? I don't know your face.'

"'I live on the other side of Atlantic Avenue.' ·

"'You must be slumming tonight. You're not a sailor, are you?'

"'No. I'm a medical student.'

"'A medical student? Then you must know....' She closed her mouth and bit her lip again.

"'Know who?'

"'Oh, no one. Come on. Let's take a walk. It's too late to stay here. Especially to sit on the ground in the dark like a lazy medical student. Pretty soon all you'll see are the lights from the buildings across the river.'

"'But they're beautiful at night.'

"'Not if you've seen them as often as I have. All I have to do is look out my window.'

"The trees were already full for the season, throwing shadows from the street lamps across our path and across our faces as we walked along the sidewalk. I wanted to turn my head sideways to see what she really looked like but all I did was kick at the small dried buds that had fallen from the trees and were scattered along the ground. From the brownstones and the red brick town houses lights glowed like open pages of a book inviting someone to look in.

"'Would you like something to drink?' I asked.

"'Sure.'

"'I know a nice bar on Atlantic Avenue where my friends and I go on Saturdays.'

"I felt her hand on my arm. 'I'm not supposed to go to Atlantic Avenue at night.' Her fingers squeezed me. 'But let's go anyway.'

"My fellow students were already gathered around the bar, some of them with their weekend dates. When they saw me, they surrounded me, their beers in their hands and laughter on their faces. I was the only one of them who had never brought a girl to the bar.

"They looked at her and so did I. I saw her face in the light for the first time. She was very young. And very beautiful. I felt ashamed of myself. But I didn't know why.

"Before I knew it, Tom's father was at our side. He was frowning at me as if I had done something wrong. He quieted my schoolmates then led just the two of us, me and the girl whose name I didn't know, to the booth farthest from the bar. 'You'll be better off by yourselves,' he said. His eyes were calm by then as if he understood. 'Stay here until you're ready to go.'"

I motion with my hand to the mirror, seeing in my mind the booths as they had been. Oh, God! As they had been. At this very moment, all I want to do is spin my head, turn it as fast as I can, get on my merry-go-round and become as dizzy as I was that first night. I want with all my heart to obliterate what's happened since, as though all those years of senseless mistakes were a bad dream forgotten in the morning...but all I do is point with my finger.

"Near where our friend is sitting," I say.

"But after my girl and I were seated in our quiet corner, hidden from everyone else in the bar, neither of us said a word. We just looked at each other. Her head was slightly bowed but her eyes looked up to me, a shy smile brightening her face.

"'What would you like?' I asked her.

"'Nothing. I'll just sit here while you have your beer.'

"What I remember most about her that first night were

her white teeth and how they contrasted with her over-red lips each time she smiled. You remember the lipstick girls wore back then? Lipstick was her only makeup. Red. Bright red. It wasn't natural on her.

"'Don't you like beer?' I asked.

"'Not really. But give me a taste.' She took a mouthful then wrinkled her nose. 'You better finish it.'

"I slid the glass along the table, discreetly turning it so that when I lifted it, my mouth covered the stain of her lipstick.

"We didn't stay long in our booth. After I finished my first beer she said, 'I must go home now.'

"'I'll walk with you.'

"'If you want.'

"When we reached the corner near where we had met, I stopped and turned to her.She took both my hands in hers. 'Thanks. I'm glad you sit in the street. I like you.'

"'Can I see you again?'

"She smiled and touched my shoulder. 'Meet me here next Saturday night at the same spot where your big feet almost tripped me.'"

The empty glass rests in my hand. The olive sits in its recess with a small pool of liquid surrounding it. I twirl the olive, watching it climb the spiral surface of the glass, wanting it to spin forever. Then suddenly, I perform my ritual. But this time, I don't allow the olive to touch my lips. Quickly, as it enters my mouth, I turn it between my teeth and bite, tasting the taste I long for. My tongue moves slowly along my lips. Was the olive a little saltier tonight than usual?

"Thank you for beginning your story. You will continue?"

"Each night until we finish."

"Then you're leaving now?"

"Remember, I must work in the morning. Thank you for talking to me."

"It was you who did the talking." She smiles and shows her white teeth. This time all the creases in her face disappear except for those of happiness around her eyes.

She stands.

"Please. Stay seated until I'm gone. Remember I must take my long hike around the room to where the corner booth used to be."

I turn to the big fellow who has been standing beside me all evening long. "Good night."

"What?"

"I said, 'Good night.' I'm leaving."

He looks at me as though I'm mad. "Yeah. Yeah. Good night."

Perhaps he's right. Mad. How many others have thought me mad? The young people around me tonight, would they think me mad if they knew me? I know my colleagues did when I gave up private patients five long years ago.

'Why are you giving up practice?' my colleagues had asked in disbelief. 'You're in your prime.'

Why? I knew why. Because I just couldn't face another patient after what I had done.

'I want to devote all my time to students,' I had said.

Of course no one has ever known. But I know. And I feel sure that she knows too.

Instead of pardoning myself to others as I make my way across the room, I only smile and nod. My smile would have pleased my mother. I can emulate a rather radiant smile. I learned it when I was young.

As I approach the woman at the table, her troubled eyes follow me step by step, and when I stop beside her, the tips of her teeth show behind her uncertain lips. Is it fear again? Or anticipation? Or hope?

But tonight I feel moved as if some wave of kindness were about to break and cover me. Could it be that memories are softening my heart or do I need others to relieve me of the story I keep repeating to myself?

I put my hand on the dry wood of her table and grasp the edge. I lean towards her. "Good night."

Tears gather in the corners of her eyes.

At the door I wave to Tom but do not look at either of my companions again.

Now the short walk home to the time of day I hate the most. At least at dawn I can hope and during the day, forget. But at night I know that everything is over and that I'm surrounded only by my own thoughts. I want to scream out loud so that everyone can hear me, scream like I did that one time so many years ago, the first time I lost the control my mother had taught me. But instead of screaming I burn my brain in agony.

'Get out of here!' I raised my hand and hit him. Was it on his face? I don't remember. I just remember my fist striking flesh that was my own and hers combined. 'I never want to set eyes on you again!' And I never did. Alive, that is. She pounded my chest with her fists then rushed to him.

At that moment something broke between us. All my burdens date from that split second of impotence—my shame, my sorrow, my inability to cope…and later, my greatest act of violence done with calm deliberation. How clean I thought I would be.

From my waiting spot on the corner I see her hair shining in the glow of the street lamp, shining as brightly as it did that first time we met with the sun setting behind her into the skyline of Manhattan.

She's walking more slowly tonight than usual. She must be tired. And now she's leaning against the lamp post. Could she be ill? Should I go to her? No. It must be the sudden heat after the air-conditioned bar. The humidity tonight is enough to weigh anyone down. There now. She raises her head and starts walking again at her usual brisk pace. I must hurry to be on my doorstep when she passes so that I can have the pleasure of hearing her heels strike the same stones that we have walked upon thousands of times.

Listen. Her heels. They couldn't be anyone else's. Her step was always strong. She always knew where she was going. Determined. Like she still is…foolishly sometimes. I swear that some day, some day soon, I'll rush after those footsteps and stop them. I will get on my knees and beg, 'Please! Please, forgive me. Let's stop this. And come home with me.'

Why have I never said, 'Forgive me?' Why have both of us given excuses for the way we said we felt when each of us knows the truth? All this acting we've done was meant only to deceive ourselves. We called it a separation of expedience. No hard feelings. 'We'll be civil,' we said. Why have we never admitted anything? Oh, God!

What fools we make of ourselves. And our shame cuts deeper when we realize the depths of our own stupidities. And what do we do? We only play games, a show in which our hearts are never revealed.

But now the sound of her steps is gone and so ends her presence for today.

The first time I entered this doorway I was awed. I never realized that anything in real life could be so impressive. I'd been invited by the Professor of Medicine, Dr. Cannon, to live in his large house with his wife and his one daughter who was still at home so that I could devote all my time to studies without interruptions. I couldn't believe what I was hearing when he asked me if I would agree to be his guest. I had never been honored as much. I accepted immediately. How gracefully I can't remember.

It was the beginning of my fourth year, my senior year. Dr. Cannon had become my ideal, the type of doctor I wanted to be. I'd spent the previous summer working as an extern on his service and, for some reason, he'd taken a liking to me. How he knew my background I've no idea. I suspect that he and his wife were lonely in the empty house with his daughter away at school all week.

The day I arrived with my books and my few belongings he invited me to join him in this parlor.

'A glass of sherry?' he asked.

'Please, sir.'

From a carved decanter he poured two glasses and handed one to me.

'Now, tell me. What are your hopes and your intentions in the profession you have chosen? And what aspects of medicine do you like most?'

Look at this parlor. Look at the heavy furniture, the dark drapes reaching to the floor. A witness to a world that no longer exists. But this parlor exists only because of me. I have preserved it just as it was as a living reminder of Dr. Cannon.

Dr. Cannon's family had built this house. They had been a shipping family who owned the wharves along the river when the area was nothing more than a village. In the middle of the nineteenth century one of the sons of the family, Dr. Cannon's great-grandfather, studied medicine and, in the course of a few years, became the moving force in founding the medical school. He was chosen as the school's first Professor of Medicine and this honor was conferred on each succeeding generation up to Dr. Cannon himself. Then, the responsibilities fell to me.

For a few minutes I'll sit in my favorite armchair, Dr. Cannon's armchair. From time to time I like to look at the one new feature of this room that I'm responsible for, Dr. Cannon's portrait done at the time of his retirement. I always called him Dr. Cannon even after we had become colleagues. 'Why don't you call me Gerald,' he had said. 'At least at home, if you must be so formal.'

Ever since that dreadful day when I acted as no honorable doctor would ever think of acting, I've had misgivings about looking into Dr. Cannon's eyes, even though I know those reticent eyes are merely paint on canvas. Their blue burns through me for having disgraced him, for defying all his principles. Thank God he was dead when it happened. If he'd been alive I'm sure that he would have suspected. More than suspected. He'd have known. His perception was like an arrow, always on target. At times we students thought he divined his diagnoses. He was a scientist I tried to emulate. But more than that, he was a man, a man who loved. It was a pity he never had a son of his own to carry on his name. Even a grandson with a different name. My name. Ha! But would Dr. Cannon have wanted my name to endure after what had happened.

Yes, I tried to emulate him. Oh, how I tried, even going so far as to ask my favorite resident to live in this house with me and my family, deceiving myself into believing that I was another Dr. Cannon. But I didn't have the character or the wisdom of Dr. Cannon. He was born with it. I tried to acquire it. And to think that Dr. Cannon introduced me to his daughter on that first weekend in September.

And here am I alone in a house that is not really mine and in a world in which I do not belong. This room, this chair in which I'm sitting, shaking with my own cowardice and deceit, were his. And tomorrow I'll play his role again. All day long I'll hear, 'Yes, professor. Yes sir. Yes, Professor.' Why don't they say, 'No, you damned hypocrite. Go to hell!'

We should all be forced to walk through the world naked with our sins and omissions showing more conspicuously than our genitals so that everyone could know what we're really like. I know what they'd call me.

Oh, God! Where did I leave that bottle last night? Next to my bed?

WEDNESDAY

I'll be late at the bar again this evening, two days in a row. As I said before, it's unlike me. A minor fault but what can you expect once decadence begins. All your good qualities start slipping away until, like mold growing over forgotten fruit, you hardly recognize yourself.

And my mother tried so hard to form my character correctly, at least the externals of character, the ones that people recognize and admire. Poor woman. I'm abandoning even those. But if she only knew what was inside me, the cancer that's consuming me, the disgust I have of myself, would she really be concerned? I hate to say that I doubt it. Since I'm still accepted by my colleagues as the honorable and admired physician that I once was, she'd have been satisfied.

Passion and jealousy are in my blood. I know that. I've slipped only a time or two and exposed them when the control my mother taught me was shattered by something stronger than myself.

'Never lose control of yourself, Peter,' my mother said.

A neighbor boy had been given a bicycle for Christmas by his parents, a red bicycle, a Columbia, with chrome handlebars and lights that could be turned on at night. I'd spent hours looking at the same model in shop windows and at advertisements in the papers only to see him parade his new bicycle up and down the street in front of everyone.

I pretended to be reading a book on the small stoop of our house, sneaking glances at him as he rode by. 'Fall! Fall!' I kept mumbling to myself. 'Break your neck and ruin the bicycle.'

When he began riding through our backyard as a shortcut to the alleyway in the rear, I could stand it no longer. One day I waited for him, crouching behind a bush that hid the garbage cans from view. Running in front of him, I grabbed the handlebars and stopped him, shaking the bicycle from side to side. 'This is our backyard!' I screamed. 'Not yours. Ours! Now, get out of here! Get out of here!'

My mother opened the window. She must have been watching. 'Peter,' she said calmly. 'That is no way to talk. Apologize and let Alvin pass by.' She came down to the backyard immediately. I was leaning on the fence with my head resting on my arms.

'Peter,' my mother said. Her hand lifted my face towards hers. 'Never forget your manners. Never lose control of yourself. Be polite no matter what happens.' She touched my cheek and smiled. 'I shall see that we have a lock placed on our gate.'

Yes, I'll be late but if my companions at the bar knew the reason why, I'm sure they'd forgive me. For a few minutes I want to think of my children and remember their faces. You see, today is the day our first child, Peter, was born. I was going to say that it had been the happiest day of my life. But it wasn't. My happiest day was when my wife said yes. I must admit she didn't hesitate at the time. We both knew what was going to happen.

No, the day Peter was born was not my happiest day, but I think my proudest one.

Pride has nothing to do with marriage, or at least it shouldn't. But when your first child is born an exaltation overcomes you that you cannot control. Irrational, isn't it? You have merely accomplished what millions of other people have but you feel mysteriously unique. Come to think of it, *pride* is the wrong word too. The word is *hope*. Hope should overcome you.

I don't have to add up the years to remember his age. I know. He would have been thirty-two years old today. Thirty-two. That's why I want to sit for a short while on the Promenade by myself and think. Think of all of them, Peter, and Reen, my daughter, and Gerald, the youngest…and especially of my wife whom I still love but cannot reach. I want only the agreeable events to enter my reverie, the early ones before their purity was spoiled. I pray especially that the last twelve years of my life will stay out of my thoughts. But I fear they might creep in. They haunt me. If they do enter my dreams I shall be forced to run to the bar. I have more protection in the bar than I do in my magnificent house.

At this time of day with the sun in the west it's impossible to find shade on the Promenade, but the touch of fresh air coming from the bay is rewarding enough. How many times have my wife and I walked along this magic path either by ourselves or with the children? First with Peter. Then Doreen was added. We called her Reen to distinguish her from her mother. And finally Gerald, Dr. Cannon's namesake, completed our little troop.

My wife, Doreen—isn't that a beautiful name?—always called Peter *Junior*. It was one of the few things we disagreed about. Can you imagine? Junior! Just to show my annoyance I deliberately went out of my way and called him Pete. Of course, both Doreen and I knew that we were playing with each other. We'd never really had a serious disagreement until.... But I said that I wasn't going to think about unpleasant things this evening. After all, today is an anniversary.

The view before me will help to cleanse my mind. People talk about the beauty of the skyline from this vantage point but I prefer the water and the way the river opens into the bay. From this distance, compared to the tightness of Manhattan, the empty plane of water looks flat and calm. Its very vastness lets you breathe and gives your eyes a chance to notice small things.

The tugboats attract me most. They remind me of tenacious students who are determined to succeed. Once this river and the bay were full of boats, but now it seems a quiet scene. Often enough, only the constant shuttle of ferries to the islands marks the time. Perhaps that's why people like to sit here contemplating the tall buildings across the water, imagining them as they look...empty, a purposeless design imposed on nature. Sitting along this stretch of the Promenade overlooking the hidden frenzy that is Manhattan, you can escape and forget what's behind you...or what you'll face tomorrow.

The sun is beginning to set over the different shaped towers. Red is tinting the sky. Time has slipped away from me and it's much later than I had intended. But I did succeed. It was a pleasant evening. I feel better. If only she had been here…my Doreen. But could we have talked of Pete and Reen and Gerald together like normal parents should? No. Oh, it wasn't all my fault. At least directly. But I was the cause of it. I'm sure of that. And what can I do now? Only get on to the bar and continue my game.

It's a short walk from the Promenade to Atlantic Avenue. From where I'd been sitting it's shorter than my walk home at night when the footsteps I'm waiting to hear are not far behind me. How I anticipate that moment. And what a mixed bag of feelings it is, both the high point and the depth of my day. Although I realize full well who she is, I wait…almost hide in the shadows on the street corner as thrilled and anxious as an adolescent. The thought of being alone with her on a dark and empty street makes my heart pound and my wild head lose its reason. I'm frightened to death. Yet, with each step I take, I cannot help but feel regret. Standing before my sculptured door awaiting her footsteps I know that the normalcy of my day is ending, that my simulated sanity will crumble with the last muted sound of her heels.

The streets of our neighborhood seem more quiet now than when we were young. It's a posher place to live. The houses are better maintained and the small gardens more decorative. Successful young people have moved into the area making the Heights approach its former glory, at least in appearance. Look into the large lighted windows if you don't believe me. These people live as luxuriously as I do.

But at night, unlike me, they're not alone.

The street is empty. I'm all by myself. The lights of Atlantic Avenue are just ahead, urging me on. But first: One turn. Two turns. Three. My counterfeit merry-go-round, my substitute for joy. My self-induced lightheadedness, like the first drink after a long day, surely the best drink of all.

'**P**op! *They've set up a carnival in the empty lot. Wait till you see it. It's better than last year's. Someone's going to jump into a tank of water from way high up on a ladder. And the pictures of the freaks in the side show are enough to give you the creeps. But the merry-go-round! What a merry-go-round! Almost as big as the one at Coney Island. Come on! Let's go. I want to ride the merry-go-round.'*

To grasp the ring. To time the approach, arm outstretched, the finger cocked. To ignore the whirl of the world outside, to see the colored lights, the blurred heads of people. It is only I who exist going round and round, accumulating a handful of rings.

But finally, the circular motion slows. Faces grow more clear. The wooden arm that supplies the rings is raised. The man holds a basket. I throw the rings in…except for one hidden in the palm of my hand. The merry-go-round stops but the calliope keeps playing on.

'Come now,' my father shouts. 'You've had enough rides for today. We've got to go home. Your mother will be worried.' He puts his hand on my shoulder, and in my pocket I clutch the golden ring I have stolen.

My father was a happy man. I know he loved my mother. And she loved him. Yet she would have liked to improve him, make him less natural than he was. But she only succeeded with me.

As I enter the bar a few of the regulars look at me. One or two

nod, then turn their heads away without another sign of rec-
ognition. I know their faces too. They're the faces I pass every
day three or four blocks from my home, strangers without
names, just faces.

How many faces are there in this world? So few of them
mean anything to us. If I look long enough at the profusion of
faces that passes me from morning till night, I begin to believe
that I recognize someone. Sometimes I feel that all the patients I have ever had follow me to this bar at the end of the
day. They change their clothes, politely fail to recognize me,
forget their complaints, and live for just a little while like an-
gels, supernatural beings whose past and whose future is now.
The light in the summer sky remains forever.

My companion, the one who usually arrives later than I,
is already at her table in the rear, her eyes more intently glued
to me than usual. She looks angry as if she had been waiting
beyond her endurance. She lifts her glass but does not drink.
Is it a mock greeting? I remember when she would look at me
with lowered lids and we would whisper.

'Have you been careful?' I would ask.

Her eyes were shy like those of a young girl. 'Yes.'

'You can't be too careful.'

'I know.' There was a pleasant roughness to her whisper
resembling the feel of a blade of grass stroked delicately from
its tip to its base.

'Please undress.' And she would blush.

She's a slow drinker. She drinks as if her glass were an
enticement and she was waiting for what might never come.

But where is my other companion who should have been
sitting at the bar before I came? I can't find her. Her place is
empty. She's always here before me. And tonight I'm later

than I was last night.

I search the room again but do not see her. Perhaps she's gone to the rest room. I'll wait a few minutes. But I don't want to take my usual seat next to hers. I just can't. It's essential that I see her first. Because she must be sitting there by herself. Not me by myself. I must walk up to her casually as if I didn't know her. After all, appearing casual is easy for me even when my heart is burning with desire. A doctor must learn to have many faces.

So, I'll wait near the door for a while. Tom won't think it strange. He knows me too well.

Standing here, not knowing what to do with myself, reminds me of the second time I brought Doreen to this bar. It was the following Saturday night, one long week after we'd first met. I'd come early with my fellow students. I just had to be with someone. I couldn't be alone before meeting her.

My friends kept kidding me as they drank beer. 'You're robbing the cradle,' one of them said. He raised his glass and rocked his beer from side to side, spilling some of the suds down his pants.

'Be careful of what you spill,' another laughed. 'You're playing with jail bait.'

Tom's father was listening to us as he dried and polished glasses. He heard every conversation that took place at the bar no matter how many people were talking. As I was leaving, he followed me to the door, the same door that I'm standing close to now. I felt his hand on my shoulder.

'Pete,' he said. He called all of us by our first names until the day we graduated. 'You're bringing that nice young girl back, aren't you?'

'Yes.'

He sighed. Tom's father had deep-set eyes, eyes that looked like a preacher's.

'I know she's under age,' I said. 'But lots of the kids here are.'

'That's not what I'm worried about. Do you know who she is?'

'No. I just met her last week by accident. I don't even know her name.'

He smiled. 'Well, I'll let you find that out for yourself. But when you come back with her, please don't stand at the bar. And stay away from the door. Go to the back booth where I put you last week. I don't want some customer to recognize her.'

Standing by the door, I'm beginning to feel as conspicuous now as I did that night. My obsession with the rest room must be attracting attention. It's impossible that the woman I'm waiting for could have been in there for so long. I'd better move to the bar before someone takes me for a doorman.

Now look at her, my lady friend at her table. She's following every step I take. Dear girl, don't you know that the claim ticket was destroyed years ago.

"Your martini, Doctor?"

"Hi, Tom. If you don't mind, I think I'll sit here for a while."

Tom is busying himself with the bartender's craft, polishing glasses, hiding what others might object to, turning imperfections into luster.

"Tom? Tell me, have you seen...?"

"Missus? No. She hasn't been here all evening."

The grinding of the door handle. I know its sound. My eyes streak along the mirror to the entranceway. Come on.

Hurry up! Waiting for someone to open a door can be like counting a slow pulse. One. Two. Three. Four. Could it be...? Damn! It's only a face, a face like all the others.

Thank God that from where I'm sitting my companion at her table is out of view, relieving me of those appealing eyes. From my angle, the mirror obliges me to see only the entranceway, a few surrounding tables, and Tom's reflection still polishing glasses.

Yet, really, all that I want to see is the door. That damned door. I can't keep my eyes off the door, the same door of years ago, a solid door with one small window at eye level. Everything else in the room is blurred as if the door were the little girl with golden hair sitting on the rabbit while the rest of the world goes spinning by.

The door is opening again. I rise off the bar stool, one foot on the floor. I see a slit of light coming from outside, a different shade of light than in the bar. Hurry up. Whoever you are, hurry up! You're slower than the last face. Do you want me to look at my wristwatch and time your entrance, take your pulse, count your heartbeat? I hear my own sigh and drop to the stool again.

"Do you remember my father, Doctor?" Tom asks.

"Remember him?" I force myself to be calm, the result of my mother's training. "Tom. Your father was a friend of mine. And a friend whose advice I respected. At times he was a substitute father to me because my father was dead."

"Did you know that he was born upstairs and lived there all his life?"

"Sure. Whenever you or one of your brothers or sisters was sick, your father phoned me. I've been to your place many times. And you and your family still live there. Right?"

"Three generations living in the same apartment. What do you think about that, Doctor? My grandfather ran this bar before, during, and after Prohibition. We're old-timers here."

The door is opening again. Each door has its distinctive sound, varying with the speed at which it's opened. Fast this time.

Tom waves at a heavy-set man, well-dressed and with a beard covering his face.

"Same people come in every night, Doctor. But once you get to know them, you appreciate them. Each of them has a different story to tell." Tom laughs. "Of course I've heard the same stories over and over again. But I don't mind listening."

I laugh too. "Like a doctor, Tom. Listening is our most important job."

"Someone's motioning at the other end of the bar. How about a glass of soda, Doctor? Something to wet your lips till you want your martini."

I turn on my bar stool with my back to the mirror and see my friend at her table. She hasn't been around this neighborhood for as long as Tom's family but she has been here for as long as I can remember. I've watched her age. Not that she looks old. She's kept up her appearance pretty well even though she no longer uses it.

What should I do? I don't want to sit here by myself guarding the door and I don't want to go to my usual place at the other end of the bar. Sitting there would destroy the effect I desperately need. That spot isn't mine unless she's there. Without her next to me would be like going home at night to the empty prison I live in.

Why not walk to the end of the room and say a few words to the poor dear girl at her table? What a beauty she was when she was young. It's a pity. Oh, I don't mean her aging is a pity. That's natural. As I've said, she's done it gracefully. I mean that all the possibilities that she has had are gone, and now she's alone.

Alone, like me? No, not quite. Despite my attempt to drown my self-pity, I'm luckier than she. During the day, my time is fully occupied teaching and running my department, although it bores me now. No, *bore* is not the right word. I'm not bored. I'm as interested in medicine as ever. But I am ashamed to be doing what I'm doing. And I'm afraid of my-self. I no longer trust myself and I go around like an informer spying on every decision I make, questioning each action, doubting my own honesty.

But unlike my poor friend, my evenings are pleasant and I can look forward to the few hours allotted me before bed-time. I have a charming woman to talk to as I drink my three martinis. I can play my little game with her and she's kind enough to play back with me. And when the evening is over I have my secret footsteps to comfort me and allow me to dream. Or is it to hope? It is only after I lock my imposing double door that the lid closes over me and all my warmth is scat-tered on empty sheets.

Look at her. My companion at the table is scrutinizing me. After all these years what can I possibly mean to her? How much does that still beautiful woman really know about me or what I'm like? Not as much as I know about her. She used to tell me everything, every intimate detail.

Oh, well. What else have I to do? Why not join her. From where she's sitting I can at least see the door without being close to it.

"May I sit with you for a few minutes?"

She starts to rise from her seat.

"I'm sorry. Don't get up. If you don't want me here, I'll go."

"Please. Sit down," she says. She lowers her lids as she has always done when I'm near.

I place my glass of soda on her table and take a chair from the table next to hers, arranging it at an angle so that, by simply shifting my glance, I can see either her face or the door to the street.

"Open your eyes," I say. I see her stiffen. Her lids flutter. Oh, dear. Did I sound too clinical again? Practiced habits, like manners, remain engraved on us forever.

She looks at me then quickly turns her eyes away.

"Please. Look at me."

She moves her glass of scotch along the table, lifts it and wets her lips. Her hand is shaking. Am I taking advantage of her just to appease myself? She has been taken advantage of enough. My mother never talked of taking advantage of people. It was how politely I treated them that mattered. But we all have desires. We all use others for some purpose or other…be it in love or with indifference. I have never been indifferent to this girl. I still think of her as a girl.

"How long have we known each other?" I ask.

"We first met when you were a student." Her voice is deeper, more uneven than when we used to talk, but still attractive. And she wears more make-up than she did, more than my companion at the bar does now. The lines around her eyes and mouth are more concealed but her skin looks thick and rigid, lending an immobility to her face. Only her eyes show a suggestion of pleasure.

I wonder how much pleasure her life has really given her.

At one time she behaved as if living from day to day was the most exciting thing in the world, teasing me with descriptions of all her different exploits. But now, behind her layers of cosmetics, a touch of pain masks her face. I think her shyness hides what she really feels.

"I'm sorry that I don't speak to you more often."

"I understand."

"Is there anything you want to say to me?"

"I can't tell you the things I used to because they no longer exist." She folds her arms across her chest holding her shoulders with her hands, covering the crease between her breasts.

The door is opening again. And there she is! The woman I have been waiting for. My friend next to me sees her too. She removes her hands from her shoulders. Her breasts lift with the deep breath she takes. I can't help but watch them rise and fall and think of how time transforms gentle hollows into ruts.

I have to stall now. I must disguise the urgency that is pounding in my heart. My timing must be perfect. Otherwise I'll feel that I have failed. The woman walking towards the bar must be seated. That's imperative. She must have her drink. She must touch the glass to her lips.

I take my first taste of the soda I have been toying with. I have never liked carbonated beverages, natural or not. Raising the glass to my lips pretending that I'm sipping, I wait, gaining time, looking my normal, calm self.

Above my glass, the woman seated opposite me is staring back, her lids taut and both hands firmly clutching the table. This time she does not look away or hide her eyes. As if in a rare moment of contact, she looks through me. Could she possibly see what's really there?

"I must go," I say.

"Yes. I know. Thanks for talking to me. I wish that I could tell you more, but I can't."

She starts to rise.

"Please. Stay where you are."

At last the woman at the bar is seated. Tom is pouring her drink. He's talking to her. I'll walk slowly in their direction.

I must restrain myself. My muscles, they're so tense. My arms feel as if they want to flap and I want to run, fly over the tables that separate us and be next to her. How could she have kept me waiting so long, robbing me of my evening.

Behind her back I signal to Tom that I'm ready for my martini. But she has caught me in the mirror. I turn my head away from her as if I'm angry, as if some stranger were prying into my affairs. Remember, dear lady, we have not spoken yet. Don't look at me! At this point we don't know each other. It is I who must force the introduction. We must use the proper formula in the opening scene. Then our lives can begin where they wish.

I turn my back to the mirror and close my eyes. Why, oh why, does time change its pace?

"Your martini, Doctor," Tom says. "Sorry I was so slow."

It takes longer to make a martini properly than simply to toss the ingredients on the rocks. Correctly shaken with the exact amount of ice and poured into a cold glass, the drink warms a little as you hold it in your hand but dilutes less. Of course, the degrees of change depend on the length of time it takes for you to drink.

I wait until Tom is gone then face the mirror.

To avoid her eyes, I use my peripheral vision to watch her. Hmm. She doesn't look quite the same as usual. She looks tired. She keeps gazing into the rust-colored liquid in her glass, disturbing the translucent cubes of ice floating near the surface with an inattentive movement of her hand. Is she thinking of something special? Will she never touch the glass to her lips so that we can meet? Come on. What else is important to me? Meeting you. Being with you.

Her small finger cocks. It's about time. I know what will happen now. She always extends her small finger before lifting a glass then tucks the finger beneath the bottom. I turn full face into the mirror as her lips part. She purses them slightly. If I were the glass, would I taste her breath?

"You have a very fine face for a woman leaning on a bar." Did I forget to smile? I must not hurry through my act like an inexperienced youth. "Or should I say that I can see that at one time it was a fine face."

"Thanks a lot."

She rests her glass on the bar. Unlike my friend at the table, the make-up of my companion next to me looks thin as if the evening had spoiled its power to deceive. Could she have gone somewhere else before meeting me? She looks more tired than I thought. Rather worn. There's a furrow between her brows.

"Smile at me," I say.

"Why?"

"Because you look sad. It's difficult to talk to someone who's sad. The conversation is too one-sided. It's like talking to yourself."

"Well, you must be happy."

"What makes you think so?"

"I see that you were talking to...."

"Yes. My wife."

"Did you enjoy it?"

I think for a minute. I felt no excitement while I talked to her. No desire. But, yes. I did enjoy it. Perhaps it recalled old times. Did I indulge in that conversation with my lonely friend at the table to console her or merely to pamper the lonely me? Had I played with her in those days too? Played with her mind? Dragged things from her simply for the superior feeling or the titillation it gave me?

"I needed someone to talk to."

"It must have helped because you forgot your glass. Look into the mirror instead of looking at me. Your glass is on her table and she's moving it towards her. She's drinking from it."

"My drink was only soda."

"What difference does that make. Tell me, did you need her?"

"I needed someone. You're supposed to be here before I am. You took so long tonight. I was anxious."

"And worried too?"

"Yes."

She looks at her glass and touches an ice cube with the tip of her finger, plunging it beneath the surface.

"I'm sorry I was late." She smiles slightly. "I didn't mean for you to worry. I was sitting on the Promenade thinking and time escaped me. I guess my thoughts ran away with me."

She was sitting on the Promenade while I was there? Where? And what was she thinking? If I had only seen her, I would have read her mind. I would have known what she was thinking.

"Anyway," she says, "I'm glad you finally had a conversation with your wife."

"That's what I'm supposed to call her. Not you."

'*S*orry we're late, Love,' my father said. 'Pete and I were walking along the river road and forgot the time.'

My mother frowned at him and shook her head ever so slightly, but her determined meaning of No could not be missed.

My father called my mother 'Love' whether she was peeved with him or not. If I wasn't noticed, her eyes would soften, but whenever she knew that I was present, she would frown at him. The stern set of her mouth meant it was not proper to use the name 'Love' in front of me, especially when it referred to her.

"**W**hat do you want me to call her?"

"Oh, call her whatever you wish."

We say nothing for a while until she leans towards me.

My heart begins to race. Please come closer. Touch me. If only with your clothing.

"Come now," she says. "Here we are at the bar, so let's enjoy ourselves. Are you going to continue the story you were telling me?"

"Of course. I promised, didn't I?"

"Then turn around and face me like we were facing each other last evening."

"Only if you look at me tonight, instead of looking at my hands." I hold my hands up between us. I want to reach for her, to take her in my arms. "You see, my hands are not the best part of me. Sometimes they do things I don't want them to."

She touches my hands and lowers them into my lap and then withdraws. For the moment, the feel of her is enough.

"Now, where was I last night?"

Last night? Or last week? Or last year? Or before? How can I possibly remember my place in this never-ending story when I play the scenes over and over again in my own mind, when events rush past me without an interval between them, without a period of rest.

"You had said goodnight to her and both of you were to meet the following Saturday near the Penny Bridge where your big feet had almost tripped her."

"Yes."

"But before you start, finish your martini first and ask Tom to bring drinks for both of us. You see, I'm encouraging you. But we're both behind time tonight, aren't we?"

I signal to Tom. He knows what the order will be. He comes only to retrieve my olive. "Everything all right?" he asks.

"Great, Tom. Couldn't be better."

"Go ahead now," she says. "Start your story. I'm anxious."

"Wait until Tom brings our drinks. I don't like interruptions. It breaks the intimacy of living the story."

I look down the bar to Tom where he's shaking my martini. Even at this distance I hear the rhythm of the ice beating at the metal, beating faster than the whirling hands of a clock striking off the seconds—and the hours—and the days—and the years.

With all Tom's skills I wonder if he can read our lips in the mirror. Or are lips backwards in the mirror too, like the signs on the stores across the street? Do words come out differently, do they mean different things when spoken into a mirror? Or are words as puzzling as the signs in Arabic, no matter in what direction they spread?

In the mirror I see my lady friend at her table looking in our direction. Is she looking at me or at my companion next to me? How can I be sure? She's holding the glass that was mine in one hand and her glass of whiskey in the other, taking alternate sips from each of them. The levels of the liquids are hidden by her hands. I turn quickly away from the mirror so as not to see her.

'*Keep going! Keep going! Keep going! Never stop! I don't want to get off.' But I feel the circles growing larger and I can tell my horse is tired.*

The end of my merry-go-round ride always disappointed me no matter how many rings I had collected because the world had stopped spinning and I could see things again as they were, as they were supposed to be. But at the height of my sobriety at the peak of the blur, when nothing could be recognized, I could choose the pieces of the world I wanted and arrange them as I wished. Only my father's face and the wooden arm that supplied the rings were real in the amorphous mass of light and shade that turned around me.

When not at home, my father smoked and held the cigarette in his mouth, one eye squinted, the fumes half-hiding his lids. He never told me how to behave but only nodded or smiled when something pleased him…or frowned. In the emptiness that is my night, sometimes I see him waiting for me in a deserted amusement park with snow falling and smoke circling his head.

'Say something, Pop. Tell me what pieces I need. I no longer have a voice in what I want.'

"**T**here you are, Missus. And Doctor, here's yours."

"Thanks, Tom."

Something tells me to go slowly tonight with my martinis. This is the second. I'm glad I started with soda if only to wet my tongue. My taste is still preserved so my evening can be full. I take a sip and look at the olive. It rolls slightly in my direction without mounting the glass or touching my lips, waiting patiently until the end.

"Go ahead, now," she says. "We're alone."

We're facing each other again. Eye to eye. Only she exists. The room can spin as it wishes and the rings can go unplucked.

"I was going to meet her the next week? Right?"

"Yes. It was to be your second date, your first planned one."

"Well, I was early and was waiting at the same spot near the Penny Bridge where I'd been the week before. But instead of sitting on the ground, I was standing. I should say I was pacing back and forth, wondering if she'd remember.

"I hardly glanced at the skyline across the river or at the bay that I loved, and I had no idea if the setting sun was red or not. For the entire previous week all I'd done was think of her. I didn't know her name or where she lived, except that she lived somewhere in the Heights. I tried to visualize her face but, in my impatient efforts, had lost every detail except for her golden hair and the fuzz glistening on her boyish legs.

"I kept looking at my watch. She was already ten minutes late. I was sure she wouldn't show up. I slumped to the ground and sat where I'd been sitting the week before, holding my head in my hands, seeing only the blurred patch of dirt in front of me.

"A pair of red high-heeled shoes stopped on the spot I was staring at and above them stockinged legs and a red hem swaying gently above two delicate knees.

"'I thought I had taught you not to sit on the ground.'

"I jumped to my feet. She was wearing a white dress with red trimming that circled short sleeves and a square-cut neckline. A thin red sash tied into a bow hung from her right hip.

71

THE EIGHTH DAY OF THE WEEK

"'You're all dressed up,' I said.

"'For you. Doctors should be treated differently.'

"'I'm not a doctor yet.'

"'You will be.'

"She put her arm through mine. The warmth of her skin made the June air feel cool. 'Let's go for a walk before you take me to your bar. Where do you want to go? Along Fulton Street to the Borough Hall?'

"'No. It's too noisy there. Let's go look at the Brooklyn Bridge.'

"'Only if you promise not to walk down to the old ferry slip beneath the bridge. I'm absolutely forbidden to go there.'

"She must have thought I was pretty dumb. I didn't know what to say as we walked along. We looked at the bridge and the lights of Manhattan from the bluff but instead of seeing anything, all I could think of was her arm touching mine and the voice I heard next to me and the white dress with the square cut neckline that I was afraid to turn and look at.

"'You know, I don't know your name,' I said.

"'I know yours.' She drew my arm closer to her and I felt the movement of her ribs. 'I heard your friends call you Pete. So your name must be Peter.'

"'But what's yours?'

"'Doreen.'

"'Doreen what?'

"She hesitated. 'Doreen Cannon.'

"Her head was tilted towards me but her blue eyes were wide open and smiling.

"'You must be...'

"'Yes. I am. So what?'

"After hearing her name I didn't want to take her to the

bar, but she insisted and waved at my friends' astonished faces as we headed towards the back booth to hide by ourselves. I had my beer, hardly tasting it as I feasted on her face and her blue eyes. After each swallow she took the glass from my hand, wet her lips, then wrinkled her nose.

"On the way home, down the silent streets I still walk each night, she laced her fingers through mine so that our palms touched and our moisture mixed. We walked slower and slower until I stopped at the spot where we had met.

"'Why did you stop?' she asked. 'A gentleman takes a lady home.' I walked her to her door praying that her father wouldn't see me.

"That summer, while Doreen was away visiting her sister, I worked as an extern on Dr. Cannon's service. Each time I saw Dr. Cannon, the image of Doreen weighed on my thoughts and I wondered how I could possibly fulfill my duties. But I must have because, for some reason or other, Dr. Cannon took an interest in me and, at the end of August, asked if I would consent to be a guest at his house during my final year at school."

"That's why you said last night that it began with her father."

"Yes."

"You admired him, didn't you?"

"More than anyone I have ever known."

Her eyes drift away from me to the mirror and, for a few minutes, only the sounds of glasses and other people's muffled voices reach us.

"Tell me. Did you admire him more than you admired her?"

"I loved her. Already I loved her."

73

She turns to me again. Her brows are raised and a wry smile brushes her lips. "Then tell me more. What happened next?"

"September finally came. One Friday night after returning from the hospital I heard her talking in the parlor. I listened on the staircase until her voice became more distinct. Then I hurried to my room.

"'Peter?' Dr. Cannon asked the next morning. 'Are you free this afternoon?'

"'Yes, sir.'

"'Could you meet me in the parlor at four o'clock? I want you to meet someone.'

"Mrs. Cannon, a quiet woman who always deferred to her husband, served tea and cake while Dr. Cannon went through the polite formalities of introducing me to Doreen. 'I hope that you will become good friends,' he said.

"Doreen and I shook hands and smiled at each other respectfully.

"After Dr. and Mrs. Cannon left us in the parlor, Doreen took both my hands in hers. 'What a fake you are,' she said. 'I'm going to tell father all about us. The truth. That we take walks together in the dark and that you force me to drink beer in a shady bar on Atlantic Avenue.'

"'Don't. Please. That'll be the end of me.'

"She tugged at my arms, drawing me closer to her. 'Don't worry. He likes you. Like I do.' She kissed me for the first time.

"'But how are we going to manage living here together?' I asked.

"'Easy. We'll lead two lives. When I'm home from school on weekends, we'll make believe and when we're alone, we'll do what we want.'"

My companion next to me seems about to laugh but represses herself by folding her arms around her chest. "It must have been hard for you to be a guest in the professor's house with your girlfriend living there? His daughter!" She chuckles. "Did you play games when the professor wasn't looking?"

"Laugh if you want," I say. "Remember, I was a kid who came from a different background. I was scared stiff."

"You never knocked on her door at night when everyone else was asleep?"

"For the first year when we were at home, I called her Miss Cannon."

"Miss Cannon. You must have been the perfect house guest."

"I was. I'd had the training. I admit that it was difficult to control myself but I persevered."

"You? Control yourself?"

"Yes. As a matter of fact, Doreen used to chide me at times for my formal behavior. 'Peter,' she'd say. 'You're afraid of my father. I know you are. You freeze as soon as he comes near you. You're like a piece of wood.'

"'I'm not afraid of him. I respect him.'

"'Warm up to him, Peter. He may be your professor but he's my father. Show some real feeling for him. Be yourself. I hardly know you when you come into the house.'

Remembering my exaggerated manners in front of Dr. Cannon, I still can't bring myself to smile while the woman beside me keeps laughing.

"The question is, did your dearly beloved Doreen know which of the characters you were playing—the innocent and gentle private Peter or the deceiving public Peter—was the real Peter?"

"Don't be funny."

Frivolity disturbs me. Flightiness and happiness are worlds apart. I know what happiness is. I've been happy many times...with my career...my work...my position. But flippancy....

Do I come to this bar simply for fun, to while away the hours, to play the little game I play each night? No, what I'm doing is not a frivolous pursuit. I need this bar. I need this martini. They are my sanity. My evenings here are serious affairs.

The olive brushes against my lips and I drink the last few drops of my martini slowly. I would like to take the olive into my mouth and roll it around with my tongue, taste the little salt that might still be clinging to it, play with it like a cat and then, unobtrusively, spit it back into the glass.

Why don't I? Just turn my head from my partner. No one would see me. It would be easy. But I can't. I'm forbidden to. For one thing, it would be rude to Tom. I know Tom doesn't touch the olive. I've watched him dozens of times. He merely pours the olive into a new glass.

My mother's voice was prim. She never raised her voice. The inflections she used were gentle, hardly differing from word to word. She rarely smiled but the composed lines of her face were pleasing no matter what she said.

'You must never be rude at the table, Peter. Mealtime, or whenever you indulge in food or drink, should be the most courteous time of your day.'

Her eyes never moved from the person she was talking to. I never interrupted her. Not once.

"**A**nd what happened next? Did you start treating the professor the same as you did his daughter?" Her hand rests on mine for a moment. She's been touching me more often lately. Is there a chance? Dare I return the gesture? Or have I become nothing but words? Thoughts? Useless immaterial things. I can only hope that my story tells her otherwise.

"Actually, it was Dr. Cannon who made it easier for me. On weekends he invited Doreen and me to his study before dinner for a glass of sherry. He encouraged us to be together. He would loan us his car, have tickets waiting for us at a theater or reservations at a restaurant. And after three years, when we told him that we planned to announce our engagement, he was overjoyed. We never had the heart to tell him that he wasn't the cause of our romance."

"And two years later you married her."

"Yes. After I finished my residency under Dr. Cannon and two years after Doreen finished college."

She's laughing again as if she finds the most romantic years of my life a comedy. "Five years living with the same woman. And unmarried. Today you'd be considered very modern."

"Don't be vulgar." I'm making believe that I'm indignant. But I think she knows it.

"I'm just teasing you. It must have been a very happy time in both your lives"

"Yes. Completely."

Our heads are bowed but our eyes are looking up at one another. A strand of her hair falls between us and she brushes it away, holding it behind her ear. As she brings her cupped hands to her mouth, the strand of hair falls again.

"Leave it where it is," I say. "I love the color."

"The color's no longer real."

"What difference does that make. I can't tell." We smile. I lift my glass but only the olive touches my lips.

"My glass is empty. Do you realize that this is only my second martini of the night?"

She finishes the liquid in her glass. The ice has melted. "And my second scotch."

"Tom." Instead of signaling to him I cry out. "Two more."

He walks down his empty pathway behind the bar and takes our glasses. "Just to retrieve your olive, Doctor."

When he returns with our drinks, Tom only smiles.

I take a long drink, almost finishing the glass.

Her hand is on my arm. I stop and look at her. Are my eyes saying what I think?

"What are you doing? Don't drink it all. Aren't you going to continue your story?"

"I've told you before that I still work during the day."

"It's not really that late."

"But to be bright in the morning, I must get as much sleep as I possibly can."

"Don't you sleep well any more?"

"Once I'm asleep, nothing wakes me...until early in the morning"

"Well then, tell me a little more of your story. Please. Not enough to keep you up past your bedtime, but a little more just to satisfy me."

A little more? How far should I go tonight? I interrupted my story when our happiness was fresh... long before I realized that I was neglecting the only thing that mattered.

I look at myself in the mirror and think of the many changes the mirror has reflected over the years...in both the room and in those who come here. Me, for example. Am I the same me that I had thought I was when I was young, or have I changed too?

After I had become a respected physician I led a different style of life than I had known before and rarely came to this bar. Tom's father understood. Whenever Tom or one of his other children was sick, he would phone me at my office.

'What are the symptoms?' I'd ask.

He would tell me.

'It could be serious. You should have phoned me earlier. I think I'd better come.'

'Use the back entrance, Doctor. It leads directly to our apartment.'

Back entrances. Used by delivery men and those who want to hide their faces or keep their secrets.

'Whenever you do something wrong, Peter,' my mother said, 'Never show it. Carry on as if nothing happened.'

My mother had given me a coin to pay the fare before we boarded the bus. The line of passengers was long and the bus was crowded, so I slipped the money into my pocket. But I kept looking back at the driver as I edged my way down the aisle.

'You kept the bus fare didn't you, Peter? You didn't fool me, you know. I could read it on your face. You need a good lesson. Give the money back to me and think of what you did.'

I look at my friend sitting at the table in the rear where our booth used to be. Both of the glasses on her table are empty. She's tilting the one that had been mine from side to side.

"She must have been beautiful," the woman next to me says.

"She was."

"She still is, you know. That's why I was jealous."

Was jealous! O minutes, hours, days…please stand still! Let this moment last forever. Tell me my nightmare is ending, that it never began, that time itself is dead.

But my martini is almost gone. My third of the night. My limit. Only a drop or two remains. And I realize that time never dies. We can't stop it or change its pace no matter how subjective we might be. Its mechanism is regulated more precisely than the spinning of a merry-go-round. Only we and what we have can die. And our progression is our end. But jealousy? O Jealousy, keep me alive!

"I'm still waiting." She nudges me with her shoulder. "Come on. Your story. You were about to enter marital bliss."

"Doreen was twenty-two when she married me. Knowing that we needed privacy, Dr. Cannon suggested that we move into his old carriage house half a block down the street. 'Young lovers want to be alone,' he had said. 'Besides you're just a few steps away and can have dinner with us when you want and visit us as you wish.'

"And we were alone. Every moment that I could spare from the hospital we were together. I soon discovered that Doreen knew nothing about housework, or how to cook. But she learned. And she learned how to love, more than just with her heart. Our years in the carriage house were carefree and natural. And when our family began to increase, we furnished the rooms upstairs.

"Peter was our first, born one year after our marriage, almost to the date. Doreen insisted that we name him after me. And two years later our daughter came along. I insisted that we name her Doreen but, to avoid confusion, we called her Reen. And two years after that, our son, Gerald. You see, my loving wife has had three children."

The air in my lungs is trapped. No words come out. I can hardly breathe. I reach for my near-empty glass but cannot bring myself to lift it to my frozen lips. I pray that I will not crush the glass into a thousand pieces.

She is staring at my white knuckles, biting her lips, showing her teeth.

A short while ago did I want time to stop to let me know that the nightmare was over? Listen to me. It's just beginning. The years fly by in front of me. I'm pushing them along, blowing wind into their sails, knowing what they'll bring. Dr. Cannon asking me to become his assistant, not appointing me but asking me first. Introducing me as his colleague. My professorship. The papers I wrote. The long hours on the wards and in the clinic. Is that what neglect is made of? Work? Or is it fatigue, that embracing narcotic that dulls our minds and tempts us with relaxation? In either case, it's neglect. That's why I blame myself. She did not begin it.

Finally, slowly, I look into her eyes. "No, I forgot. She has had four children. One later in life."

Why didn't I forget to mention that last child? Why didn't I allow my lungs to explode? Why did I bring that up when everything was going so well? Why do I keep flagellating myself? Do I need constant pain to remind me? Do I enjoy my guilt? Do I have to inflict it on others to enjoy it even more?

She looks down into her lap. Her words come slowly. "Three would have been enough."

I see only the brow of her head and a few loose strands of hair hiding her face and touching her breast. I turn and look into the mirror, into the backwards world that shows me more.

She's frowning at her glass. She wipes at the corner of her eye with the tip of her index finger.

"Yes. Three would have been enough," I say. "Women should have children when they're young. It's tougher when they're old. They don't expect them."

"I know. As you get older, or as you doctors say, 'in later life,' women don't know what to expect. They only know what they want. Especially when it's not given. Any diversion comforts them."

I swallow the rest of my martini and place the glass on the bar. The olive rests in the bottom.

"Please excuse me," I say. "I must leave now."

"Don't forget your...." She motions with her head towards the table in the rear.

"No. It's the least I can do."

"And this time, say good night to her. We all deserve that. A good night is more truthful than a good morning."

She calls after me. "Don't you want your olive?"

Without turning to see her sitting there alone, I say, "No. Not tonight."

The distance from the bar to the rear of the room seems longer than usual. My friend at the table follows my weary steps across the uncrowded floor. What must she think about all of this? As I come nearer, the expression on her face gradually changes until it assumes the same old frightened look that I remember. Had she looked at all the others that way too? Or only at me because I knew everything about her?

"Please don't look away," I say. "I want to tell you something."

I had never told her much when we were younger. She was the one who talked to me. She was always patient, waiting for hours if I was late. After leaving the hospital I would knock on her door.

'Is that you?' she would whisper.

'Yes.'

'The door isn't locked. But be quiet.'

She moves the glass that had been mine away from her as if offering it to me, her blue eyes never leaving mine.

I bend so that my head is level with hers. "I just want to say I'm sorry."

She backs away, her brows knotted in confusion. "But why?"

At the corner of the street I stop, take a deep breath, and think of what a long night this has been. If I had only met my companion on the Promenade earlier in the evening. I would have told my story differently in the freshness of the air coming from the bay. The birth of my oldest son would have been the climax and she could have helped me celebrate that happy day so long ago. Yes, he would have been thirty-two years old today.

When I was thirty-two, Reen was born. When she was a youngster she followed me around like a devoted kitten. I don't think we ever had a disagreement. I never raised my voice to her. But then, except on rare occasions, I never raise my voice to anyone. I had been taught not to.

What I meant was that Reen always tried to please me.

'**D**ad. Tell me about your day. How many patients did you see and what was wrong with them?'

'Now a young girl doesn't want to hear things like that.'

'I do. Because I look up the diseases in your books so that

I can remember them. I've even made a list of all the ones I know about. I can recite it if you want.'

Reen and I had a rapport with each other that went far beyond that of a father and daughter. Even when I grew careless of my duties around the house and spent less time with the children and my wife, Reen and I remained good pals. I think she had the same awe about medicine as I'd had when I was young. After all, it was in her blood on both sides. She looked like her mother but she acted like me. Whom does that make her take after? I like to think it's character that counts rather than looks…. No. I frequently use incorrect words. I should say *characteristics* rather than *physical appearance*.

But what about the boys? Whom did they take after? And that last one. Whom did it take after? Not me. I'm sure of that.

Here she comes. The one I'm waiting for. I see only her hair as she passes through the lamplight. But I know that it's she. If I deliberately let her see me and walk to the Promenade as I did earlier in the evening, would she follow me? At this time of night we could sit on a bench and be all alone, our heads together with her hair resting on my shoulder, brushing against my face, smelling as it used to in the clearness of the days we were together.

Now, I rarely have the chance to share the pleasures of the day with her. And never the pleasures of the night. I have only my games to play. I'm forced to do with the little I have and, I guess, be thankful. Guess? I know. I am thankful, but I want more. I have always wanted more. I want her back with me.

Listen to me rave. And I consider myself a logical man…if such a quality as logic can exist in man. How can I possibly have two different feelings at the same time? A moment ago I was bitter. Bitter about the creature that was born when she was forty-five. Now, a few seconds later, more than anything else, I desire the one I was bitter about. My mind spins constantly. If only I could forget what I don't want to remember.

'Look at the little girl in front of you, the one on the rabbit, and you won't feel dizzy.' My father had been right. But when I regained my balance and lost my fear of dizziness, I wanted to be dizzy. And I never was again. I had to pretend to be dizzy by turning in circles.

I must hurry along. I don't want her too close behind me as I walk home. I don't want to hear her footsteps until I'm opening the door that is rightfully hers, the door that she walked from the first night we met, the door I feared would open the first night I brought her home, the door that confines me at night to my madhouse.

I hear them. I have trained my ears to detect the first and last perceptible sounds. With my forehead resting against the door their resonance is more distinct. Louder. Louder. They are building to their peak. She is near me, near the foot of the steps. But wait! The rhythm falters. The footsteps have stopped. I dare not turn around. Could she be thinking of joining me, ending my long imprisonment? But no. The footsteps start again and soon are gone. Good night, my love.

Each time I lock the door behind me I look into all the hidden corners of the hallway as if expecting someone to appear. Perhaps a guest, perhaps someone who has lived here before? One of her family I never knew? I have yet to see anyone but some day I may start hearing their voices. I would welcome voices…an interruption to my own sad sounds speak-

85

ing mutely to myself. I might even learn to talk back to the voices I hear.

A meek voice says to me, 'Are you the professor of medicine, the professor that all the students admire?'

'Yes, I am that self-made man, the man who started with nothing and ended with fame.'

A deep voice this time. 'How about your father-in-law, a really great doctor.'

'I admit he taught me all he knew. But advances have been made since his day.'

A feminine voice. 'Come now. Without marrying his daughter you would have remained a nothing.'

'But I love her! Bring her back to me and I'll become a nothing again.'

I can shout in this hallway all I want. 'I love her! I love her!'

See. No one responds. No one hears me.

Oh God! Listen to me. What am I doing? I must stop these self-imposed delusions or I'll get that bottle before I should.

Almost every night, to gain a little time and to clear my head, I walk around this mausoleum of a house and choose a room to sit in before going to bed. Tonight I choose the library where I used to study when I was a guest of Dr. Cannon's.

About eleven o'clock he would knock gently on the door. He never entered until I said, 'Come in, please.'

'Peter. You need a break. I have brought cocoa and a sandwich for us to munch on before I retire. We can talk a little.'

'Thank you, Dr. Cannon.'

He might talk of medicine or of his travels and the years he spent in Vienna studying or of his family, whom he called merchant sailors. He never stayed more than ten minutes.

'Now, Peter. Don't stay up past midnight. If you try to cram too much into your head at one time, it becomes waterlogged.'

Look at all these books around me. How many of them have I read? How waterlogged have I become?

'*What are you reading, Pop?*'

'*Books that bricklayers read. Guys that don't know nothin'. But you'll be different, Pete.*'

When I was a boy, except for a few school texts on the desk in my room, we had very few books. In the first place, there would have been no place to put them. The few that we did have were next to the radio. I remember my mother's copy of Emily Post, although she hardly needed it. My father had a Bible that he read once in a while and every week he bought the Saturday Evening Post. He never went to the public library but belonged to the lending library at the corner drug store. Except for the rare occasions when he went out for a beer at night, he read in the kitchen after my mother was in bed.

And after he had finished one book, he would come home two weeks later with another bricklayer's book to read until his bed-time.

Many of the books that surround me here in Dr. Cannon's library taught me what I know and how to cure the ill. I have no doubt that my father planted the seed of medicine in my mind when I was young and very impressionable. But I have always believed that I possess some inherent qualities that would have made me choose the profession anyway. I dislike what doesn't work. I dislike any deviation from the normal.

When I was a boy I used to mend things, fix other children's toys if they were broken. I wanted to see them whole again.

I like to think that is why I became a doctor. I wanted to make everything right. *Perfect*, my father said. When I treat a patient I like to believe that I can repair something that is wrong or, at least, alleviate suffering. I can't abide treating the hopeless. And that's what that creature was. Hopeless.

What a nightmare of a time I lived through back then. Even worse than now. Fifteen months in which everything went wrong...and then the aftermath in which I still exist...a less severe but a longer-lasting pain. And it all started with this hand of mine. Look at it. The hand that examines patients, writes prescriptions, gestures when teaching students, and at one time...it seems so long ago...made caresses of love. It all began when I struck our first-born son. Everything changed at that instant and the snowball started downhill. And I was inside that snowball, inside a blind merry-go-round spinning and rolling in all directions until six years later my confined reason shattered on the rocks of an imbecile.

I must get some sleep. I know how to.

THURSDAY

This afternoon the dean and I discussed my retirement. A year ago when I confided in him that I had decided to retire early he begged me to reconsider. The mild hypertension that I had developed over the past few years was unimportant. God knows, with the state I get into sometimes, it should be higher. What worried me was my attention span.

I was having difficulty keeping my mind on the affairs of the department. I relegated as many problems and decisions as possible to others and, later, when they discussed them with me or sought my advice, I had forgotten what the problems were about. Sometimes on rounds with the residents and students, I lost track of my train of thought. While I fumbled with the patient's chart, stammering a few incoherent words, I could see the puzzled looks on the young men's faces.

Not that I feared that something was happening to my mind or that I was displaying the first symptoms of Alzheimer's. But I was losing interest. I wasn't keeping up. I knew it.

The week before I had told the dean of my decision to retire, the senior resident had asked me to read the final draft of a research paper that he and I were presenting at a meeting. Of course he had done all the work, but as head of the department my name would appear with his on the article. When I read the paper I hardly understood what he was talking about. That convinced me. It was time to quit.

Over the course of the year, from a position of opposing my retirement, the dean now fully agrees with my decision. Perhaps he has been talking to others. But he has found a good way to profit from it. He has planned a banquet and a formal ceremony in December when my wife and I will be honored, where my name and the Cannon name will be linked forever on a bronze plaque in the lobby of the hospital. Officials like occasions. But I don't care. At least it will give me the opportunity to take my wife's arm in mine and sit next to her at a dinner table.

This evening I'm on time. In a way, I'll welcome the air-conditioned bar. After the comfort of my office, the heat was unbearable driving home in the traffic. If I dressed a little more appropriately for summer and learned to take off my tie before leaving the hospital, perhaps I'd feel cooler. But, somehow or other, I feel undressed if my neck is showing.

'**A**lways look your best, Peter,' my mother said. 'A good appearance impresses others.'

My mother was very fussy about my clothes. Although our circumstances were modest, my mother always insisted on buying the best.

'Not only do good clothes fit better and look better,' Peter, but they last longer.'

Yet her special delight when shopping for me was the one item of clothing that was seldom seen: Handkerchiefs. I had more of them than I could possibly use. Her taste was for soft white cotton. When she passed a display of handkerchiefs, she couldn't resist stopping, smiling at the saleslady, and feeling each sample between her fingers, her eyes showing her displeasure or approval.

'This is a nice handkerchief, isn't it, Peter?'

'Yes, Mom.'

'We'll buy it.'

And when we arrived home she carefully placed the new handkerchief in my drawer next to all the others. My mother ironed my handkerchiefs perfectly without one edge overlapping another.

Well, here we are. The table at the rear is empty as it should be when I enter and my companion at the bar is seated in her usual place. She doesn't try to look at me. Again as it should be. After two days, our timetable is back to normal.

This evening I have no need to rush. Besides I'd like to digest, at least part way, my hospital cafeteria dinner. So I'll spend a few minutes standing at the bar…but not too close to that man in the pin-striped suit.

I really don't like to strike up conversations with strangers. When I'm forced to be near someone I don't know, a nod or a smile suffices as a sign of good will or, if I recognize the person, a greeting for courtesy's sake. People I meet by chance usually have nothing important to say. They're full of idle talk or, worse, they want to know too much that is personal, asking questions I prefer not to answer. Besides, I come to this bar for a specific purpose.

"Hi, Tom."

"Good evening, Doctor. Shall I make your martini?"

"Not just yet. But have it ready when I move down to my usual spot."

Both of us look towards my companion sitting at the far end of the bar. Only the man in the pin-striped suit is between us. He looks younger than he did from behind. How come I missed his face in the mirror? I see everything in the mirror.

He turns his head, not to look at me but to look at the door. Those hollow cheeks and the small pointed nose look familiar to me. And the tic—winking his right eye then lifting his right shoulder slightly. I think I know him. He couldn't have been a patient of mine at one time?

"Tom? Who's that fellow just down the bar from us?"

"I don't know. He's not a regular. But every couple of weeks or so he comes in, orders a tequila straight, then sits there sipping it and watching the door until a friend arrives. Once the other guy comes they put their heads together, take notes, and slip envelopes to each other. They talk so low that I never hear a word they say. And when it's dark outside, they leave. I suspect they're bookies. Frankly, I'd rather he go someplace else. But it's none of my business."

"I've seen him before."

"I can't imagine where, Doctor. He's not the friendly type."

"Just out of curiosity, I'm going to say hello to him."

"Good luck, Doctor."

I move down the bar and stand next to the man. He takes no notice of my presence but, looking past me, glances quickly at the door.

"Good evening," I say.

His head turns. The muscles around his right eye twitch and his shoulder jerks.

"You look familiar," I say. "Perhaps we've met somewhere."

His tic again. Three times in a row. He picks up his glass with his left hand and brings it to his mouth without swallowing. His eyes look through me as I watch his tic. A red tip of a tongue slides across his lips. "I don't know you, mister. And you don't know me." He turns away.

"Perhaps not."

"Definitely not," he says without looking at me.

As I walk towards my companion, I watch his bent head and his pin-striped suit in the mirror. He drains his glass quickly, leaves a bill on the bar and heads towards the door.

Tom brings my martini. "I don't know how you did it, Doctor. But you sure got rid of him. For good, I hope. He looks like a bad actor to me."

"You sure were right about him not being the friendly type, Tom. Just being near him made me feel uncomfortable. But I could swear I've seen him before."

"Maybe in the movies," Tom says as he moves away.

"You don't have to be in the movies to be an actor, Tom."

I could have said, 'Take me for example. What kind of an actor am I? Watch the way I glance in the mirror waiting for my partner's first sip while feigning disinterest.'

I know exactly how to do it. After all, I've played the role often enough. Tom knows our little game. He goes along with us, playing his role too…the perfect barman. We all learn a role to play no matter what we do.

And there's my cue. She touches the glass to her lips. For tonight's performance I want to be a star.

"You have a very fine face for a woman leaning on a bar." I smile.

Am I allowed to improvise? May I say, 'Your face is the finest I have ever seen. I want to hold your head between my hands, caress the warm skin of your cheeks and bring your lips to mine...never, never to be separated?' But, I am forbidden. I must be content with the lines I have.

"Or should I say that I can see that at one time it was a fine face."

"Thanks a lot."

What's wrong? Her voice is flat, without inflection, floundering in her mouth.

"May I sit with you?" I ask.

"Please. The stool is empty."

Please? At this point she's supposed to be aloof, a bit scornful for having been approached, not solicitous.

In the mirror I see a look of horror on her face.

She holds her shoulder with her hand and puts her lips against her wrist.

"Is something wrong?" I ask.

"Yes."

"Are you ill?"

"No. No, it's not that."

"Please, tell me."

"That man you were talking to. He frightened me."

"You know him?"

She closes her eyes tightly and her teeth bite her wrist. "Yes.... Oh, not really. I met him once. Years ago. He was younger then but I'd never forget that face."

"Who is he?"

"A friend of someone I knew. Someone I loved."

"What does he do?"

Between her clenched teeth, she groans, "He's a pusher."

Pain shatters my knuckles as my hand strikes my son's flesh and my head rolls with my own screams. 'Get out of here! I never want to set eyes on you again, you goddamned druggie!'

Pete's blood dripping down his shirt. Doreen rushing towards me. Stopping a foot in front of me. Pounding my chest with her fists. Crying. 'What are you doing? Have you no heart? No feeling for him?'

I hear her words over and over again, sniping at me during the day, haunting me at night. Because what she said is true. In one instant, without thinking, I ended his life and mine. My son. Our first-born. Each time that scene recurs I see him as I first did, an infant in the hospital wrapped in a white blanket, his eyes still closed, sucking at his mother's breast. I was embarrassed by that. Can you imagine a doctor embarrassed? Embarrassed at the normal? Embarrassed by his own son?

As I stand here at the bar ashamed of my impotence, his first blanket and the last shirt I saw him in become one, covered with the red stain of our child's blood. Now I remember that bastard who was standing at the bar. I had seen Pete meeting him on the street corner, talking to him, walking away with him.

I search the mirror to orient myself, to find out where I am. Outside, the street is the same as ever. At the far end of the bar Tom is talking to a customer. My eyes drift past the faces at the tables until they reach the small table in the rear.

My lady friend is sitting there. I missed her entrance again. She's looking at me as she always did through eyes that never smile. If I could see her face more clearly, I'd know what she was feeling. She used to understand.

'I'm sorry,' I whisper to myself. 'I'm sorry.'

Is that all I can ever say? 'I'm sorry.' Must I keep confessing to myself, repeating the words over and over until I think that no other human emotion exists? Can't I get it through my thick skull that sorrow relates only to events of the past, dead events that can no longer be lived. I want to stand on the top of a mountain and scream, 'I'm sorry' for the last time, and then live my life again.

I swallow my martini in one shot. One bite on the olive. I hardly taste it.

I feel her hand on mine. It stays there. Her fingers are cold. "Don't make matters worse," she says. "Help me forget that face."

"I can't."

"Please try. Perhaps if you continue your story."

"What I say won't help. From now on, the story becomes one long sad affair."

"I don't care. Sadness is part of life and I want to hear your voice. I need to hear your voice."

I motion to Tom. His eyes show the same concern his father's did on that first day he led me and the young girl whose name I didn't know to the hidden booth.

"Just a martini," I say.

"What happened to your olive, Doctor?"

"I forgot myself."

He bows his head. "Some ice for Missus?"

We say nothing to each other until Tom returns. My eyes are closed. I cannot bear to see the mirror.

"Please," she says. "Your story. We're alone now."

"I'll try. But remember what I told you. From now on, you'll discover what I'm really like."

"Don't say that. Just continue."

Slowly, my mind drifts back to a happier world, covering my wounds with the dust of more pleasant memories. "Let me retrace my steps a little and tell you again of our children, Peter, Reen and Gerald. Okay?"

"Yes."

"Well, you must turn and face me then. The way you're supposed to when I tell you stories."

Her eyes are looking at our hands when she turns. I haven't the courage to ask her to look at me.

"All of them were born while we lived in the carriage house."

"'The most carefree years of your life,' you said." Her voice is less tense. I feel her palm move along my hand.

"Yes. And the happiest."

"Why?"

"Because we were together and had time to play with the kids as a mother and father, and to play with ourselves as a husband and wife. Dr. Cannon still ran the show at the school so all I had to do was follow. As for Doreen and me, we lived from day to day and week to week in our crazy little house without a care in the world.

"And it was a crazy house because in those years, carriage houses weren't considered quite the proper place for a young doctor with a family…at least in the Heights. Most of the old

97

carriage houses were used as garages or workshops or sometimes by an artist."

I hear her sigh. Her shoulders rise a little but I see only her crown of hair. She's still looking at our hands.

"Close your eyes for a few seconds and maybe you'll see it."

"They're closed," she says. "Describe it to me."

"The house was set back from the street with a short driveway paved in red brick leading to a large stable door. Our entrance was to one side of the stable door and the window of our front room on the other. It was a rather drab looking building back then, nothing like the renovated carriage houses of today of brightly painted brick with iron lanterns and window boxes full of flowers.

"To brighten the house, Doreen planted the narrow strips of earth on each side of the driveway with evergreens and blooming vines so that color greeted us all year long, even through the snow. We parked our car, the first we owned, inside the stable doors where the carriage used to be, and our rooms—only a narrow living room, a small bedroom, and a kitchen—were arranged around our inside stable like a letter U. For a while we were a little cramped but after Reen was born we redid the upstairs and had more space than we needed.

"If Dr. Cannon hadn't asked us to move back into the town house with him after Mrs. Cannon died, I would have been content to live in the carriage house forever."

"And your children? Tell me about them. I'll keep my eyes closed and maybe I'll see them too."

"Pete, Reen, Gerald. One right after the other. All within four years. We didn't waste our time back then with unimportant things.

"Pete, the eldest, became the leader of our little mob. He'd organize the other two into games or projects and tell them what to do. And they'd do it. He was like a little mother to them. He had something planned for each birthday or holiday and the three of them would work on it behind our backs, thinking we didn't know. I still have a desk drawer full of polished stones and decorated plates that they made and all the childish notes they scribbled."

Her eyes are open now looking into mine, appealing for me to go on. I look away, not into the mirror but at the glass my hand is reaching for. I take a sip to clear my voice.

"Pete was Doreen's child. He adored her, following her around the house when he was small and spending all his spare time with her as he was growing up. Just as I did back then. So I couldn't blame him. If anything went wrong, he'd run to her.

"Whereas Reen was just the opposite, running to me when she'd see me leave the house:

"'Dad, where are you going? You're not going out now, are you?'

"'I've got to go to the hospital for a few hours.'

"'When are you going to take me there?'

"'When you're a little older.'

"You see, I had two beautiful women who were always trying to please me.

"But Gerald was different, a strange mixture of affection and independence. He was a quiet kid. As he got older, we'd find him in the library lost in a book of poetry or on the Promenade by himself staring at Manhattan and the harbor. Not on a bench but on the pavement, even in the coldest weather:

"'What are you doing there on the ground?'

"'Looking at the sky, Dad.'

"'But it's too cold to be sitting there.'

"Doreen squatted next to him, peering at the Manhattan skyline we knew so well. 'What do you see?' she asked. 'Is there anything different?'

"'There's something different every day, Mom.'

"'Show me.'

"'Do you see the building with the green pointed top?'

"'Yes.'

"'Look at the color of the sky surrounding it. See the purple with a trace of pink in it? You can almost smell it, it's so fresh. You only see that color when spring is coming. And it changes every day.' He jumped to his feet and reached for Doreen. 'Give me your hands, Mom. I'll pull you up.'

"Gerald could describe the color of the sky for each season of the year and how differently the buildings looked, gay or somber, or retreating on the cold gray days of winter, or blossoming upward in the summer sun.

"Our lives were full back then." I turn my head from my companion to conceal the tightness in my voice, and in the mirror see the signs across the street with the inverted letters I can't decipher and the Arabic scrawls I've never understood. "Yes. Our happiest time. Until, somehow, it slipped away."

"Why did it slip away?"

I take another sip of my martini, just a small one. The olive hardly moves.

"I don't know."

"You must know. A man of your intelligence."

I laugh. "Perhaps I didn't use my so-called intelligence. Or perhaps I had become too impressed with it." This time the olive touches my lips.

"Please. Turn around and look at me. I want to know why your happiness slipped away. And I want to see your eyes as you tell me."

My *merry-go-round is spinning as if my mind has regained its reason. Everything around me and all I know is blotted out but in the blur of the crowd I make out one face, not my father's but the face of Dr. Cannon. As my painted horse goes up and down and the calliope blares its good news, I reach for the ring I want and from Dr. Cannon's hand I receive the golden keys.*

"Yes," I say. "I know why. Or at least I've found excuses. When Dr. Cannon retired, the department became mine and I was determined that my standards would surpass even his. Was I jealous of him? Of course not. He was my hero and I wanted to imitate him. Oh how I wanted to be him. But I had to work like hell to accomplish what I finally did and my hours of labor showed. I forgot that Dr. Cannon was Dr. Cannon and that I was merely me. A difference in mettle, genes, if you want."

"Don't be a fool."

"Yes. His strength was natural. He was born with it. Mine was grafted on...and the graft didn't quite work."

"You're too hard on yourself."

"Don't I deserve it?"

"Deserve it?" She throws my hand that she has been holding into my lap. "Just because you were different from the man you admired? Why should that stop your happiness with your family?"

"Because I was afraid of my own weakness. Once I had my position I had to keep it, hold on to it with my claws. And

I could keep it only through work. Everything else became secondary because my work was me. At times it wore me out. Sometimes when driving home alone at night, I wanted to run and run and run until I was back where I belonged."

I glance up at her but her head is turned away. I can't look into the mirror to find her because I haven't the courage to face where my eyes will lead me…to the rear of the room and the other woman sitting at the small table waiting for me as she did when, in the depths of my weariness, I needed her.

"Instead of spending my spare time at home with Doreen and the children, I went out of my way parading myself before all the meetings and conferences I could find, important ones or not. Being seen and heard by colleagues was paramount. I wanted to be known by everyone.

"Oh, I was clever about it, displaying my knowledge behind the veil of modesty my mother had taught me, appearing as the humble protégé of Dr. Cannon while I strayed further and further from what counted most.

"'Did you forget about yesterday?' Doreen asked me.

"I thought for a moment. It had been a beautiful June day and I remembered seeing the children arranging tables in the garden.

"'Was it something special?' I asked.

"'It was Junior's birthday. We waited until it was almost dark. He was very disappointed.'

"'I'm sorry.'

"'You should think of us once in a while.'

"'Everything I'm doing is for you.'

"'Is that what you believe?'

"Things like that happened over and over again…canceling weekend trips to the beach or a ski resort, forgetting anniversaries, birthdays...including Doreen's.

"And all that I could say was, 'I'm sorry.' Facile words, *I'm sorry*. Words without guts.

"Finally, it sunk into my dull brain that something was wrong between Doreen and me, not by realizing that my own conduct might be at fault but by seeing Doreen's attitude change...nothing obvious except to me. The playfulness she had always had was gone and her spontaneous fits of silly love became nothing but a memory.

"So, thinking that the problem was simply the amount of time I spent with my family, I tried to remedy the mess by devoting one weekend a month to Doreen and the kids no matter what my schedule demanded. And every summer Doreen and I took a two-week vacation by ourselves. You see, I thought I could recapture in two weeks what took years to lose."

"Did you recapture anything?"

"In a way. At least we had short intervals of fun. We pretended."

I twirl the olive in my glass but it settles again to where it had been, trapped by its own insignificant weight. I think to myself, how often have I had fun, real fun, where nothing else mattered? To have fun I need to be light-headed, dizzy. My mind must go spinning off to someplace else and leave me behind. Like my merry-go-round. Like Doreen when I first knew her. The kids when they were young. I don't know what real fun is...natural fun.

Doreen was different. She was never as serious or intent as I was. Or should I say, never as dull as I was.

I'm laughing and my companion is smiling at me.

"For the first couple of years we went to a ranch, a place

of my choosing, a setting as divergent from Brooklyn as I could find. Can you imagine, a ranch in New York State. And the name: The Bar-B-Q. Corny, isn't it? It was really a working farm, a dairy farm with only a few guests. Doreen laughed herself silly when she saw lariats hanging from pegs in our room and cattle skulls on the walls and especially at the two of us dressed in boots and Stetson hats. As she undressed that night, she tossed her clothing on the horns of the skull above our bed and kissed me. 'The Boots and Stetson Ranch,' she said. 'B. S. Ranch, for short.'

"The wide open spaces. Life in the saddle. But let me tell you, the first time we went horse back riding I was scared stiff. Buck, the man who owned the farm that he called a ranch, took one look at me and saddled a tame old mare. Doreen galloped off and, turning to wave me on, saw her frightened husband clutching the saddle horn for dear life.

"'Where did you learn to ride?' I asked as she led me back to the stables.

"'In Prospect Park when I was a kid.'

"'I never knew that.'

"She turned from me and placed her cheek against the horse's muzzle. 'There are lots of things we don't know about each other,' she said."

At her table in the rear my other friend is writing. Now, isn't that unusual. She puts the tip of the pencil in her mouth, pauses, removes it, then takes a sip of scotch. She seems to be choosing her thoughts carefully. Perhaps in her old age, she's becoming a lady of letters. What a look she's giving me. Staring straight at me then jotting down words in her notebook. My God, I hope she's not writing her memoirs. That would be amusing. She was always free in what she said and never hesitated using names. With all my other problems, a best seller would serve me right.

When she and I were on closer terms than we are now, she would come up with the most outlandish ideas without ever losing the serious look that was on her face.

'Do you know how to stand on your head then flip into bed on your back?'

'No.'

'Would you like to learn?'

'No.'

'Well, let's think of another trick.'

Time with her made me forget myself. Despite the nonsense she talked, or maybe because of it, I became lost on the spinning make-believe world I loved where my surroundings, if only for a little while, did not exist and I could face tomorrow again.

But how can I face the rest of the story I'm telling? What I can admit to myself, I find impossible to admit to others.

'Indecency is vulgar, Peter,' my mother said. 'Proper people do not like it. Always act as if you were modest.'

The idea of nudity always struck me with terror. While dressing in a locker room or at a public pool, I hid myself behind a towel or sat with my knees touching, hiding what my mother called my private parts. I don't know why. As far as I could see I was as normally developed as anyone else. But I didn't want others to know, to see me as I saw them.

Once when I was a kid at the pool, one of the other boys grabbed my towel as I was taking off my swimming trunks and threw it to someone else. There was a free-for-all, my towel flying across the room from one kid to the other. At first I ran after it, completely naked, trying to retrieve it. As the laughter grew I walked back to my locker and dressed without drying.

"You've been thinking for a long time," my companion says. "Are you going to go on?"

I finish my drink, this time remembering to leave the olive in the glass.

"Yes. But let me order first. Do you want another?"

"No. I think I'll stay with this one tonight."

After Tom leaves, she slides my drink along the bar and sets it next to hers, just out of my reach. She smiles at me. "Go ahead now."

I smile back. Others who didn't know us might think we were a happy couple talking of the insignificant happenings of the day. And maybe we are.

"Well," I say, "for years Doreen and I acted as a normal husband and wife, like others in our social class. Successful. Content. Thinking of the children.

"The kids grew up. We went to their graduations, gave them parties, met their friends. And I worked as hard as ever. I grew rather proud of myself. My initial apprehensions of being unsure proved to be unfounded. I knew my way.

"I had chosen my staff carefully. All of them were more than capable. And I made sure that friendliness and harmony existed in our working group. I could depend upon them. And I must say, without boasting, that they thought highly of me. I was pleased. I had tried to imitate Dr. Cannon all the way and succeeded...professionally."

I look at my glass more than an arm's length away but I am too polite to reach in front of her.

'Never reach, Peter,' my mother said. 'Ask someone to pass what you want. And always say, please.'

But I've reached. I'd practiced with the rings, hadn't I? And I'd gotten them.

'Try for two,' my father said. 'You can do it.'

And I usually got two. Three rings were more difficult. Only rarely did I come up with three.

Perhaps if I said 'please' now, I would get the third ring, the chance I long for most? The one I let slip away...by reaching for something I had no need of, something I already possessed.

How could I have let my life slip by without realizing what was important? How could I have gotten so mixed up? As my view of values grew more and more distorted, I ignored my own symptoms and was blind to the signs of my own disease.

Why am I incapable of saying the words I should when it comes to those I love? Is it pride? Am I still ashamed of my own nakedness when I'm quite aware of what I look like? Of course she knew what I was doing. How could she help but know. I knew she knew.

I see my olive sleeping in the bottom of the glass, motionless, losing its salt. A hand's-breadth is so far away.

"And what did your wife think about all this?" She looks to the woman sitting at the table in the rear and closes her eyes. "Tell me about her."

"Unless one tells you what they're thinking, you can only deduce it by their actions."

"Did she tell you?"

"No."

"Did her actions change?"

"Not that anyone could detect. But if you had known her.... Walking along the bluff. Crossing the Penny Bridge. Sitting on the Promenade. Alone with her in our carriage house. Yes, our personal life was different. You know what they say about enthusiasm waning?"

"Too well."

"Since necessity spares few of us, we fell into a routine."

"Did you no longer love her?"

"I have always loved her. From the day I touched her shoulders near the Penny Bridge and saw her hair."

It is I who turns away. Does love sleep like a seed in winter? Must it constantly be reawakened? Did I have to destroy love completely to make me want it more? Or is love just a figment of my imagination, a mirror in which I see myself? I close my eyes hoping that I will spin and spin and spin, stay on my merry-go-round forever. Answers are clear when the world is a blur.

"But now you live apart."

"Yes. Our relationship grew worse. Remember, I warned you that sadness would enter my story."

"Your story was already sad enough."

"Sadness can be like an incurable disease, progressing from one inalterable stage to the next."

I open my eyes and see my martini still sitting before her. She doesn't touch the stem to offer it to me even though she must know I need it. My martini will be warm before it does its work. But I cannot bring myself to reach.

"It was an emotional outburst that made matters worse," I say. "An emotion as uncontrollable as love or sadness. It was anger...on my part."

'**A**lways *control yourself, Peter,' my mother said. 'Never let your feelings show.'*

Which feelings did she mean? All of them?

"**L**ove. Anger. Sadness. Aren't all three somehow related?"

She doesn't answer me.

"Tell me. Are they related?"

She merely looks at me then bows her head to the bar and rubs her hand along its well-aged surface. The defiance in her eyes is gone.

"Do you want me to go on?" I ask.

She nods her head without looking at me.

"It concerned our oldest son, my namesake, Peter.

"After two successful years at the university, he just stopped. I couldn't believe what was happening. He spent days away from home and, when he did return, talked in riddles then went to his room.

"I tried to reason with him. He refused to say a thing. All I would get was a flippant remark and what had become his favorite refrain, 'You ain't with it, Dad. You're passé.'

"At first I was more frustrated than mad. What he was doing was inconceivable because I wanted Pete to be me. Me, all over again. To follow in my footsteps. To have the interest in medicine that his sister, Reen, showed.

"'Doreen,' I pleaded. 'What are we going to do?' I slammed my fist on the table then hid my face in my hands.

"She ran her fingers through my hair, something she hadn't done in years. She knew all my weaknesses but she had never seen me really mad before.

"'Whatever we do, we can't lose control of ourselves,' she said. 'That will only make matters worse.'"

Was I hearing my mother's voice again? Was I back in my boyhood house receiving advice? Would my father take me to the carnival on Saturday? Would I ride the merry-go-round and forget everything I had ever heard?

How I long for that drink that is so close to me. The color of a martini is like the color of cool water. If you poured it into a tall glass and took the olive out, no one would know what you were drinking.

"Now here comes the funny part."

"Don't!" my companion says. She still isn't looking at me.

"Do you want me to stop?"

"No. But please don't say the story you're telling me is funny."

I hesitate for a minute. The words I'm going to say run through my mind like a film I've seen hundreds of times.

"At the time I had a resident, Damon Sutherland, whom I admired very much. Trying to imitate Dr. Cannon again, I invited the young man to live with us, partly for his own sake but primarily for the good influence I thought he would have on Pete. To my eyes, the difference in their age was negligible.

"From the time Damon had joined my service, it was obvious that he would be a first-rate doctor. He was smart, but more than his intelligence, his diagnostic acumen was incredible for his age, reminding me of Dr. Cannon's uncanny ability to know what was wrong with patients. No hint of superiority or arrogance ever entered into his behavior with other residents or students, and when he dealt with patients he was genuinely sympathetic without allowing his sympathy to interfere with his objectivity.

"I thought his presence in the house would help bring Pete back to us. But Pete took no interest in him, ignoring him when they were together, mocking the young man behind his back for his natural good manners, manners so unlike my fumbling ones at the same age."

I look into the mirror, stealing a glance at my friend next to me. She's still polishing the smooth surface of the bar with her fingers, back and forth, back and forth with the forbearance of a woman waiting for her next labor pain, a sign that she can scream legitimately.

"Doreen was the one who told me what was wrong with Pete. I suspect that Damon must have been observing him and confided his opinion to her, too diffident to approach the professor himself.

"We were in our bedroom undressing for the night. Pete hadn't shown up for dinner that evening, a not-uncommon occurrence but one that always upset me and made me brood. Doreen sensed the bad temper I was in. She knew the slightest alteration of my mood despite my increasing efforts to hide things.

"She took both my hands in hers reminding me of forgotten evenings when we sat on our favorite Promenade bench talking of how we would shape our lives. I could feel her fingers stroking my palms. 'I think I know what's the matter with Junior,' she said.

"I sighed. 'What?'

"'He's taking drugs.'

"'Drugs!' I sat on the edge of the bed. 'Drugs?' To me it was inconceivable. 'What for? What does he need drugs for? Things like drugs don't happen to people like us.'"

My companion is looking straight at me now. "And what did you, his father, do?" she asks.

"I tried to talk with him."

"Talk?"

"An argument."

"Tell me about it. What did you say?" Her body moves towards me, tight as a cat's ready to spring. "Tell me exactly what happened."

During my lonely hours at night when the only sound I hear is my own heavy breathing, this scene spawns the beginning of my pilgrimage that has yet to end. Every day that passes adds to my burden, making it more difficult to bear. When my worn-out mind sees the three of us, Doreen, Pete and me, I can at least endure the torment of what is about to happen, but now that I must describe it to the woman next to me in words, will it drive me mad?

"The next day, soon after I arrived home from evening rounds, Pete finally showed up. Doreen and I were alone in the parlor. We hadn't said anything to each other for ten minutes. The intense silence was unbearable.

"'Hi, old timer.' Pete saluted me with a defiant flick of his fingers without even looking at me. He walked to where his mother was sitting. 'How are you, Mom? Sorry about last night.'

"I jumped to my feet. 'I want to talk to you,' I said.

"'Can't you see I'm talking to Mom, old feller?'

"'Well you can turn around and talk to me, *young feller*.'

"'All right, Doctor. What do you have to say?'

"I half ran to where he was standing next to his mother. I shouted into his face, 'You're on drugs! Aren't you?'

"'Did that diagnostician you brought into the house tell you that? I've seen him watching me. He has a vigilant eye, you know.'

"'You goddamned ungrateful ....'

"'Thanks for the compliment, old timer. But what I do

away from home is my business…just like some of the things you do away from home is strictly your business.'

"*Get out of here!*' I screamed."

My companion's face in the mirror is nothing more than a blur, rippling like water flowing away. I can't possibly say another word. Words tear scars apart, making old wounds bleed again. Words drag on and on, prolonging my vision, making my shame cut deeper.

"And?"

I look at her. At the torment in her eyes and the deepening lines around her face that I can see more clearly tonight. If I could touch that face, would I forget? If I could put my finger on her lips, would all our words cease to exist?

"And?"

"I hit him."

Her eyes snap shut. Her upturned face looks old, pale.

"And?" She sighs as if all her breath were lost.

"I never saw him again."

We are silent. I cannot hear a sound in the barroom. The lines around her eyes relax into a painful frown and she covers her face with her hands.

"It was a cold winter," she mumbles to herself.

"Yes."

"Ice covering everything."

"Yes. I'd slipped and fallen myself."

"Were you hurt?"

"Just a sprained shoulder and wrist. My resident, Damon, had to drive me wherever I went."

"Drive you? Yes. I'm sure."

She lifts her face from her cupped fingers and her words become distinct and sharp. "But tell me. I want you to tell me what happened after that."

"Nothing. I had no idea what happened to Pete until three months later. Doreen, Gerald, Damon and I had just finished a slow Sunday lunch because of my painful shoulder. Reen was away at college. We retired to the parlor where I was reciting to Damon all of Dr. Cannon's accomplishments and the influence of the Cannon family on the school when the phone rang. Doreen answered it.

"'Water Street?...A warehouse near the Manhattan Bridge?...The fifth floor? You say there was a party?'

"Absently she replaced the phone repeating once again, 'A party?' Then she turned and looked at me. She said nothing but her arm began to raise as if she were going to point her finger.

"'Who was it?' I asked.

"'The police.'

"'What did they want?'

"'Junior is dead.'

"No one spoke. Gerald fell into the nearest chair, his eyes as blank as if he were staring at the skyline of Manhattan from the Promenade.

"Then Doreen began to wail, 'No! No! No!' Damon rushed to her side. She turned to him, fell against his shoulder, and began to cry. He held her in his arms."

Sitting in this bar, the strange scene that flashed before my mind at that awful moment becomes as vivid as it was then. As if the words I had heard and the actions I had seen had never happened, I saw myself as a boy again living in my parents' house looking out the front room window at the heavy poplar tree hanging over the street. Every year the tree had become taller, stronger, shadier, until it resembled a solid green wall.

In the morning, on his way to work, my father would wave to my mother and me as he passed under the tree until the tree seemed to swallow him from view. One evening he was late for supper, something that rarely happened. His one beer at the bar was timed to my mother's plans. I suspect that he had met some old friends that evening and instead of one beer had a few.

The next morning my mother said nothing to either of us. She walked brusquely around the kitchen scraping her feet along the linoleum then served my father his bacon and eggs. As he was leaving she said, 'I hope that you can make it home tonight.' She refused to go to the window with me to wave at him.

That afternoon we were informed that the scaffolding on which my father was working had broken. .

The poplar tree keeps growing, its still leaves hanging limp, as it envelops Doreen crying on Damon's shoulder, his hand pressing her closely to him, until I see them no longer, while I stand spotlighted in the blazing sun.

I am overcome by choked-up tears. The lights of the bar sparkle. The mirror, like a river capturing the sky on a spotless day, blinds me with its reflections. I look at my companion. Her face is pale, drained of life as if she had fainted. Was my story too much for her? Her mouth is sucking at the air but her eyes are dark as if she were searching for something she will never find, something that she has already lost.

She turns from me. I reach in front of her and grab my drink, swallow my martini fast and bite the olive. She's slipping something into her mouth.

"What are you doing?" I ask.

"Nothing."

"Is there something wrong?"

"No."

"But you put something into your mouth."

"Just an aspirin." She takes a deep breath. Her hands grasp the bar. "A slight headache."

"You can swallow pills without water?"

"They're flavored for children."

Her head remains turned away. But she makes no attempt to chew.

Should I touch her? Put my arm on her shoulder? Ask her to look at me?

Bits of the olive cling to my teeth. One piece is soft. I feel the pimento but cannot tell the taste.

Finally she turns to me. Her eyes are filled with fear turning their blue into gray. "You had better go." She tries to smile. "It's late."

"Have I frightened you? I'm sorry."

"No." She shakes her head impatiently. "And stop saying you're sorry. All of us are sorry." I feel her clammy hand on mine. "I want you to continue your story tomorrow."

"I don't know how to."

"You must."

She moves my hand to her knee holding it against her dress. "And don't forget to say good night to...."

"My wife."

"Yes. You've been neglecting her tonight."

I dare not look back as I cross the room. My hand that has touched her is pressed to my lips tasting what little scent is left of her.

Instead of having to bid good night to another part of my past, I would rather walk along the streets with my eyes closed until I was standing at my front door waiting for the sound of footsteps. Like being on the merry-go-round, I want to obliterate all visions and all words so that I see nothing of the now or the then or what I know will follow me into my disheveled bed, tossing me until I drop exhausted into my self-induced oblivion. I just want to hear footsteps, the click of heels, the monotonous repetition of sound while I pray for something new to happen.

My companion at the table is watching me. Her lips are parted as if to speak or to touch her glass or to feel another's lips with her own, but her blue eyes are shaded by a tender frown. She closes them and bows her head as I approach.

"Good night," she says without looking up. "I hope you sleep well."

"Thanks. I'll try."

Outside, in the humid air of the street, I lean against a wall as I wait for the woman I want to appear beneath the lamp light. I can hardly stand. I'm tired. Telling my story of each nervous scene to my companion at the bar has worn me out and thinned my mind with a sense of unreality. I only know where I am and not where I have been.

That voice, the voice shouting into the face of the poor ignorant young man who was my son, could not have been my voice. I had been taught never to raise my voice. The fist, ready to strike, must have been another's hand and not the hand of a healer like me. Watching my favorite resident assume my role to comfort the woman I love had to have been an illusion. The slow motion of talk convinces me that my story could not have happened. Someone! Please! Tell me it did not happen.

'I want you to continue your story tomorrow,' my companion said. Why does she want to hear the rest of my story? If I could cut it from my brain and bury it, I would. But I know that it has taken root and will squat in the midst of my thoughts for the rest of my life.

Continue my story tomorrow? How can I when I must tell her of the pain that Doreen inflicted on me and of the years of brooding that warped my mind to conceive the act I finally committed, an act not conditioned by a wild melange of love and anger as when I struck my son, but by hate and volition.

But, her hair glimmering beneath the street light, her face hidden and bent as low as mine tell me who I am. I must hurry and precede her.

My brow rests against the sculptured wood of my door, my eyes closed, my heart open to the miracle I want to happen.

Oh, God! Please make her hurry. She's so slow tonight. What could be keeping her? Should I count seconds from my memory of time? Look at my watch? Turn my head? She couldn't have passed by without my knowing it.

Time is standing still, taunting my expectations into despair. Doesn't time know that the moment I hear her first steps is the most precious moment of my day, the hour I wait for, the point in my life where everything could change? Yes. Change. Surely, she is as tired of her life as I am of mine. Why else would we revert to games?

I hear them. Her steps. They're slower than I thought. Worse than slow. Faint. Their thrust is gone as if she were walking on sand.

Pressing myself against the door, I listen more intently to the sounds that are hers, feeling as close to her as I did on nights when my head rested against her breast, hearing the beat of her heart.

Her skin smells clean. My lips touch her flesh, moistening her desire with my swollen breath. We whisper each other's name, we shout from our mountain tops until the long night dwindles into sleep.

But no. Her footsteps do not stop. Nor do I turn and run after her. Tonight is not the night. Yet I refuse to believe that the pattern we have established is immutable. I know that it will change. Soon it will change.

An old lock has a solid sound when you turn the key. It glides smoothly, resonating like a low-pitched tympanic roll from distant drums. The door swings noiselessly on its hinges, then shuts, isolating me from the world. Again, I'm completely alone.

Alone. I say that every night. Why? By now, I should be used to myself and all my dreary excesses.

Absently, I walk up the deeply carpeted stairs, imagining my silent footsteps are hers walking beside me. Trying to prolong my last few moments of calm before entering the bedroom that had been ours, I catch sight of the door of the children's room, not where they slept but their playroom.

When they were young, warnings in childish lettering were always taped to the door. 'Private.' 'Keep out.' 'Beware to those who enter.' On rainy days or in the evenings, Doreen and I knew exactly where to find the kids until more adult amusements enticed them elsewhere.

Forgetting their past warnings, I open the door. The air smells stale. No one has entered this room for a long time. Even the cleaning lady has avoided this forgotten place. I run my fingers along the dusty desks, tall books, photo albums.

They were Pete's. He was an enthusiastic photographer when he was young.

I reach for an album at random. Flipping the pages, I see Doreen standing in the backyard in a light summer dress, the type of dress I was most fond of. She's holding a flower close to her face, her mouth half hidden by the petals, her eyes looking past the cameraman. Another photo of Doreen talking to Reen and Gerald. And still another of Doreen waving from the car as we were leaving on one of our silly two-week vacations that I thought would mend our deteriorating world. Behind the driving wheel I see the shadow of myself.

Pete hated those trips we took, being without his mother in the middle of summer. As Doreen and I planned our two weeks, he grew more and more sullen, walking past us in the parlor, making sure he was seen.

'Why do you want to go away, Mom? Let Dad go by himself like he does to most of his meetings.'

Yet he always took a photo of our grand departure as if recording something he wanted to forget. Before the car started, while Reen and Gerald stood by the roadside waving good-by, Pete would turn away. I remember him when he was fourteen trying desperately to hide his tears as Doreen called his name and threw a kiss.

I open the final album, curious as to when Pete's last photos were taken. Below each photo, in his carefully controlled hand, Pete printed the date, the place and the names of the people. On the fourth page of the thin volume I see faces of classmates and names unknown to me taken during his first year at college, only two years before he died. And then, empty black sheets of paper.

Quickly I walk to Gerald's desk. His chair is as dusty as

the albums. But I whisk at it with my handkerchief and sit where he would sprawl with a handful of papers before him, thinking more than writing. Sneaking a look in a drawer, I pick up a small notebook written in his scrawling left-handed script.

This river is my road to walk upon
Leaving ivory towers to the sky
I search the dust of long dried lakes
To tell me of the reasons why.

Whatever is he talking about? Gerald was a strange boy. He was always trying to figure out what everyone else ignored or took for granted. I can see him staring at a plant in the garden, dissecting it with his eyes or gazing absently at the sky completely oblivious to the rest of the world.

'Stop daydreaming, ninny,' Pete might say. 'And help me move this box.'

'You moving a box?'

'What does it look like I'm doing?'

Gerald would jump up and give Pete a hand, joking about himself at the same time. 'Just thinking of what's coming up for dinner.'

Perhaps Gerald was too honest to accept the world as we do. Even as a kid he displayed the same sensitivity to things as Dr. Cannon had. He could perceive how people felt by the way they smiled or simply by the way they breathed just as he could tell what the smallest sign in nature meant.

When I could spare the time, I took walks with Gerald more often than with the other kids, not because he was the youngest but because, as Pete and Reen grew older, they were more involved with affairs of their own. The Promenade was our favorite place. The skyline across the way with the water dancing in the sun or escaping from the lights of night bewildered me and calmed my thoughts.

'Do you see it, Dad?'

'See what?'

'The tide. Look. It's resting. Soon you'll see it swell then rush the other way.'

After Pete died Doreen ignored me when we were by ourselves which I could understand. But with others around us her cold acceptance of me broke my heart. Only the attentions that Damon, my resident, paid to both of us compensated for her indifference.

'Mom,' Gerald said one evening when Doreen and I were reading in the parlor. 'You and Dad ought take a trip together like you used to.'

An intense silence gripped the room. I looked at Doreen, never suspecting what was going on. She was holding her breath, her face scarlet, her hand pressing her abdomen as if she might be ill.

She stared wildly at Gerald. 'Why?'

'Because you and Dad should be together more often.'

Why do I feel calm tonight? It makes no sense. I should be more provoked than ever. But in spite of the story I must tell tomorrow, I have a premonition that something will change, that the mad state of my existence will be altered. Each night I hear that message drumming in the footsteps as they approach. Soon I will either follow them or they will stop and come to me.

I draw the covers of the bed on my side and light the

lamp above my head, feeling the unbalanced gloom of shadows casting their spell on the empty space beside me. At one time, as if by some secret plot, two lights were extinguished simultaneously while our separate warmths mingled in the dark.

The bed looks neat now, but during sleep pillows will be crumpled and covers thrown in disarray. I have spilled my bottle more than once.

'Never let others know your thoughts, Peter,' my mother said. 'Keep them to yourself. Then you'll retain control.'

I wonder what the cleaning woman would think of that as she makes my bed.

Just a jigger tonight.

It's surprising how good whiskey tastes when you don't really need it.

FRIDAY

Although not a drop of rain touched me, today's pervading drizzle soaked me to the skin, reminding me of my last visit to Seattle and the last time I saw my daughter, Reen. People tell me that Seattle is an ideal place to live. After four years of working there, marrying a colleague and having a child, Reen, I'm sure, will stay for good.

This morning I received a letter from her. In her crisp style, concise and rather blunt, she described the responsibilities of her appointment as an instructor on the medical school staff. Rereading her letter during the day, less for her news than the opportunity to think about her, I could visualize Reen from the time she was a kid running along the Promenade to the day she received her medical degree, always sure of where she was going. How happy I should be, I thought. At least something in my life has worked out. And at least I have a grandchild.

But I'm not happy. In my thoughts, Reen has almost ceased to exist. A terrible thing to say, I know. But it's true. For me, presence is what counts, not words written in a letter or the hollow sound of a voice over the phone, but presence. The faintest change of mood revealed in eyes or the slightest variation in the movement of a face or a hand tells me more than what a person says.

How can I justify my disappointment in Reen when she's doing exactly what I wanted her to? Yet I cannot help but think that choosing Seattle for her training was an escape from what she thought she knew.

When she returned from college to enter medical school and live with us again she found an empty house, a house where her parents led separate lives. What a shock that must have been. Poor Reen could only speculate about the truth. But if she had asked, who could have told her? Each of us, Doreen and I, had picked our favorite pieces from that fragmented pile we called the truth without ever trying to discuss our problems.

Ordinarily Reen is direct. Right to the point. If you didn't know her, you'd think that she was callous.

'Dad, I want no help from you at school. Consider me as just another student and don't talk about me with your fellow professors. They already know I'm your daughter. So be tougher with me than with my classmates.'

'But Reen....'

'I want no favors, Dad. Except to learn from you.'

One evening when we were alone in the parlor during the Christmas break of her freshman year, she asked me, 'Dad? May I move into the carriage house?'

'Now why do you want to do that? You've just come back to us and brightened up this lonely old place.'

'Thanks for the compliment, Dad. But I'd feel better living down the street by myself. Don't worry, I'll be with you often enough. Probably more than you want.'

Although she had said nothing at home, I had watched her growing discomfort during those first few months she lived with Doreen and me. After all, I thought, she's still a young girl with the simple ideal of following in her father's footsteps and has yet to know the tough hide she'll eventually develop practicing medicine.

On more than one occasion, I had observed her studying Doreen's last child as if she were studying a specimen. The child was already two years old. It hadn't yet learned to walk but lay quietly in its crib with wide-mouthed unconcern of its surroundings.

I'm sure Reen suspected her mother. No one had ever talked openly about the affair but what had happened was common knowledge. My colleagues on the faculty were discreet.

'Dad. Why don't you institutionalize that child?'

'I don't think your mother would approve.'

'Have you talked to her?'

'No.'

'Why not?'

I shrugged my shoulders.

'Because you're afraid to, Dad. Can't you see that it's ruin-

127

ing your lives?' She took my hand as she used to when she walked with me as a small girl. 'You can forget how it happened if you want to, Dad. But you can't forget that child. There it is, forever in front of you, keeping you and mother apart...even if you do forgive her.'

Forgive? Me, forgive? Oh, dear child. If you could clear my head...or if I could clear my head...or if anyone could clear my head, I might know whom to forgive.

Reen was perceptive to feelings if not to motives. She was a senior medical student when the child died. She said nothing at the time but by then she was well aware of what the clinical course should have been. Shortly after, when I announced that I was giving up private practice, I could tell from her look what she was thinking, not a look of reproach, but worse, one of pity.

'I've accepted an internship in Seattle,' she said.

The bar is jammed tonight...the way I like it best. The motley drone of voices says that the weekend has begun. Who cares about rain in July? Who cares that we have to shout to be heard? Who cares? The world is inside this bar and what goes on outside is something to be forgotten. Well...at least forgotten until Monday when the reality of one's self will again be diluted by necessity.

Tom waves and I motion to him to mix my drink. Among the weekend crowd, I recognize several faces that are more distinguished looking than the rest.

I bump into someone, a neighbor from down the street, not a good friend but an acquaintance. "Sorry," I say. "But I must get to the other end of the room."

"Good evening, Doctor." The eyebrows rise as much as to

say, 'What is a doctor doing in a neighborhood bar?' Then he looks at my companion whom I'm longing to be with. Do I see the man shake his head in everlasting disbelief?

Of course, he's right. I don't believe it myself. What does a doctor…I was going to say a respected doctor…need with a neighborhood bar? For me, the answer is simple: To meet a woman. To patch a hole that has been cut into my heart. To play a game. Perhaps to start all over again from the place where I began.

This bar was the beginning of my cure, not my downfall. My downfall is me and what I'm made of. I'm addicted to myself and I know it. I need someone to help me. And that someone is here. If I can't have her I shall rave as if the clear-headedness of night has no end. .

Only my merry-go-round will help me then. I shall stay on it forever, spinning around in my self-made stability while laughing at the dizzy world standing still beyond my blur. Remember, I have never been dizzy since childhood unless I make believe I am. My secret is to keep my eyes on one real thing, something to stare at and think about for long hours on end, never allowing it to escape my mind.

'**L**ook at the little blond-headed girl sitting on the rabbit,' my father said.

'Never show your feelings,' my mother said.

'Always get two rings, but try for three,' my father said.

'Good manners pay higher dividends than grades.'

Oh, God! My poor parents. They were trying. I love them for how they tried. I'm trying too.

"**G**ood evening, Doctor."

129

"Good evening."

"Don't you remember me?"

I look carefully at the man. He's about my age and wears a necktie as I do.

"I'm afraid...."

"Don't be embarrassed, Doctor. We met only once a few years ago at the time of your child's death and then very briefly. I work at the registrar's office at Borough Hall."

The face? No, I don't remember it. But the registrar's office? Yes. I had signed the death certificate myself. Viral pneumonia was my diagnosis.

For some reason, I take the man's hand and shake it. "Nice to have seen you again," I say.

Tom is placing my martini next to where my companion is sitting. I see only her back and the smooth lines of her shoulders flowing from beneath her golden hair. Again I wave to Tom as I elbow my way to the bar. And then I behold her in the mirror.

Did she catch sight of me in the crowd? She must have. She brings her drink to her mouth deliberately, her small finger tucked beneath the glass as if the slowness of her motion were designed for me alone. Her lips pout and her calm face tilts ever so slightly.

That's my signal. I move next to her.

But suddenly her body stiffens! She's turning away. I see only the back of her head.

Nevertheless I bend towards her, my mouth close to her ear.

"You have a very fine face for a woman leaning on a bar." But she makes no response.

This time I shout. "You have a very fine face for a woman

leaning on a bar."

She is glowering at me as words dwindle from my mouth. "Or should I say that I can see that at one time it was a fine face."

"Shut up," she says. "Do you see her?"

"Who?"

"The woman next to me. She's pregnant."

"So what?"

"And half drunk."

My companion jumps from her stool, almost upsetting my drink, and takes a step backward. A girl in her twenties and about six months pregnant is looking despondently into her glass, twisting a ring on her finger and muttering to herself.

An elbow digs into my ribs. "Call Tom."

I signal and Tom hurries towards us. Before he can open his mouth, my companion motions to the girl next to her. "Take a good look at her, Tom. I'm surprised you served her."

Tom glances at the rounded abdomen sitting in the young woman's lap. "Sorry. Guess I missed her. Never saw her before."

"Missus," Tom says politely, pointing to a notice behind the bar. "You know that in your condition, it's unwise to drink. The notice warns that..."

"I don't give a damn what the notice warns," the young woman snaps.

Tom hands the notice to her. "Here. Read it. It says drinking can affect your child's brain."

"Let it. I'll do what I want. Besides, this thing's mine. Not yours." She tilts her head and empties her glass.

"Sorry. But if that's the way you feel, I'm not serving you."

"Then the hell with you! I'll go someplace else."

Both of us are silent as the girl stumbles her way through the crowd until we lose sight of her.

"I know it was none of my business," my companion whispers. "But...brain damage...."

"I understand."

She moves to the young girl's stool. "Here. Take mine. There's nowhere else to sit tonight."

Her hands remain folded on the edge of the bar while her eyes never leave her glass. In the mirror, I try to avoid her thoughts, searching instead for safety in the faces of the crowd. She sighs and shakes her head ever so slightly.

"Come now," she finally says. "You must continue your story asyou promised me last night."

"I told you then that I didn't know if I could."

"You must. I have a right to know how you feel."

"Feel?" I laugh. "Then or now?"

Her eyes soften as she touches my arm. "Well, first tell me how you felt then."

I take a long drink of my martini, the first taste of the evening.

"Drink slowly," she says. "You have more time tonight. Tomorrow's Saturday."

"Have you forgotten? I also work on Saturday."

"In any case, sip your drink." She points to the mirror. "But look. Here comes your... Eh, what shall I call her? Your other friend? You almost missed her. For a man whose profession depends on observation, you can be terribly inattentive. Now turn around and nod to her."

"Why?"

"Because you owe it to her. All of us should pay our debts."

Walking to her table, my other companion looks at me, her face dancing past the medley of heads between us, her expression more enigmatic than ever.

During all those years that we were intimate she puzzled me, giving what she had no need to and asking for nothing in return, as if she pitied me. I raise my hand in a feeble greeting and then hide it in my lap.

"At least that's something," my companion next to me says. "Now you can start your story."

Before me in the mirror I see all the bewildering things I know—my friend alone at her table sitting where she sits each night, the signs in the street outside, my aging face with its full head of black hair.

"Come on," she says. "Forget the mirror. We're supposed to look at each other. Remember? Those were your rules."

"Yes. That's what I want. But I'm a little afraid."

"There's no need to be afraid any longer." She rests her hand on mine.

What I'm about to say I would most like to forget. I'm ashamed of it. Not so much at what was done but at myself for having been so ignorant, never realizing what I had already thrown away and lost.

"Okay, I'll try." I wet my lips then twirl the liquid in the glass, concentrating on the olive until it settles where it should be.

"Well…after I had lost my self-control and hit Pete, Doreen never behaved the same towards me again. I couldn't blame her. I thought time would eventually heal the wound. But after Pete's death all my illusions vanished. Not that we argued openly. Indeed we hardly recognized each other's presence, acting as if our minds might break if the other spoke.

"Damon, my resident, became our mediator, encouraging us to say a few words at dinner, to bid each other 'Good morning' and 'Good night.' In other words, to be civil."

Closing my eyes I see Damon coming from the room that Doreen had moved to, approaching me with his instinctive bedside manner like a doctor giving a progress report to the next of kin. 'She's fine. Nothing to worry about. Go on to the hospital and I'll meet you there later.'

"Were those months hard for you?"

"Impossible! Civility never works. It's too shallow. We'd have been better off without our pretense. Better to scream our heads off at each other, say what we thought, show our feelings. Then we might have known exactly what the other felt…and maybe have had a chance to start again."

I play idly with the stem of my glass massaging its erect shape between the tips of my fingers. "In medicine, unless you know the cause, you rarely cure a disease. Neither of us really knew why our befuddled reasons acted as they did. We said the polite things we were supposed to and then we parted, Doreen to her room and I to what had once been our room while Damon soothed us both. I felt so indebted to him at the time that at every opportunity, I thanked him profusely."

Her hand is on her shoulder, her eyes shut tightly as if trying not to see.

"Open your eyes…please."

"Give me a minute."

"I must see them if I'm to continue. They tell me what you're feeling. They help me."

Slowly, her lids part and her tired brows ease into a smile.

"Is that better?" she asks.

"It'll give me strength."

"Then please go on."

"Ever since then I've often wondered why I didn't simply say to Doreen that I was sorry, that I shouldn't have hit Pete, that I should have tried to help him. It would have been easy. Inside, I was very contrite for what I'd done but I never confessed my feelings, allowing them instead to burn all traces of understanding from my mind. I don't know if I was afraid or just too ashamed of myself."

Her eyes are listening to my every word, waiting faithfully for the next.

"We're stupid, aren't we?" I have the courage to touch her knee, to feel the smoothness of her stocking.

"Yes."

"You see, I didn't realize how deeply Doreen had been hurt. I don't mean at the loss of Pete. That was the ultimate tragedy. But hurt by me over the long years of…well…neglect, if you want to call it that. She must have grown to hate me.

"Yet, throughout that painful period when I felt so confused and helpless, Damon was always encouraging.

"'She's coming along,' he would say. 'Pretty soon she'll forget all of this and things will be back to normal. Just have a little patience.'

"Something must have been apparent at the time that didn't register with me. But Gerald must have known. Looking back on those months, I remember his quiet behavior at the dinner table, how his eyes traveled from his mother to Damon while his own innocent face said nothing. In the evening when we pretended to read in the parlor, Gerald would excuse himself and leave the house.

"One night after Doreen and Damon had retired, and I was trying to sort the maze that had become my mind, Gerald appeared from nowhere and fell into a chair opposite me."

I laugh and let my hands fall on the bar.

"What are you laughing at?" she asks.

"Gerald. What a kid. Had his own way of doing every-thing. The way he sat…like a bunch of rags. Whether he was at the table or on the ground looking at the sky over Manhat-tan, his body just seemed to collapse and there he was.

"'What are you doing here at this time of night?' I asked him.

"'Just came back from a walk.'

"'On the Promenade, I bet.'

"'Yeah. It's a good place to think.'

"'And what were you thinking about?'

"He pulled his chair closer to mine. 'About all of us.'

"I said nothing but simply looked at him.

"'You may think I'm still just a kid, Dad. But I do under-stand things even though I can't figure out why they're hap-pening.'

"I must have gasped at the sudden realization of how ob-vious our family dilemma had become even to a boy like Gerald because I remember the distinct sensation of cool air on my lips and the flow of saliva in my mouth. 'Gerald. For someone who's going to start college next year, you're too serious. At your age you should be having some fun.'

"'What were you doing at my age, Dad?'

"'Studying. I wanted to be a doctor.'

"'I'm studying too.'

"And then he kissed me goodnight, something he rarely did, and left me alone in the parlor.

"Surrounded by the trappings of another age that I had refused to alter, I wiped my eyes so that I could see the por-

trait of Dr. Cannon. Dr. Cannon who could find his way
through the most difficult of problems. 'Use your eyes,' he
would say. 'And then your reasoning will follow.'

"And then I realized that Doreen was pregnant."

I finish my martini and let the olive sit between my upper lip and the rim of the glass, wanting to take it into my
mouth and chew it slowly, crushing the soft flesh between my
teeth.

In the mirror behind the bar I look to the far corner of
the room and visualize the booth where our lips met for the
first time. I can still feel the moisture and smell the perfumed
flavor. Was that really a kiss? Our first kiss? Touching my mouth
to her lipstick on a glass of beer? But how am I to know? I
have forgotten what a kiss is like. I have forgotten the thrill of
another's moisture mingling with my own. I have forgotten
what she tastes like.

Despite the mass of people, the heads separated from bodies, the disjointed arms lifting glasses to awaiting faces, I see
my other friend with her full red lips sitting at her solitary
table. As long as I have known her, her lips have been over-
done.

'Why do you paint your lips so red?' I had asked her.
'And make them look so large? Your lips are beautiful just the
way they are.'

She was in her slip standing in front of a mirror redoing
her make-up.

'I need them red. And I need them large. They help me
survive.'

'Why couldn't I...?'

'No. We've been through this before. I won't let you.'

How many rings did I want? And what good are rings, anyway? When the merry-go-round was slowing to a stop, when my mirage faded into faces and the world again recovered, I had to throw my rings into a basket. I never knew how many I had grabbed. In the excitement of snatching them from the wooden arm, I always lost count. Only once did I steal a ring, a gold one. I still have it hidden in the lower drawer of my desk. Sometimes I remove the papers that cover it just to put my index finger through the hole and think of my father and mother and the little apartment that we shared.

"Should I signal to Tom?" my companion asks.

I let the olive slip back into the glass and shake my head 'Yes,' afraid to say a word.

We wait in silence. Tom takes our glasses and leans across the bar. "I talked to the young girl as she was leaving. She seemed more reasonable. Said she'd go home." He smiles at us. "I think she will."

I feel her head against my shoulder and in the mirror see the changing color of daylight in the street outside and my indecipherable signs glowing into a deeper red as if the sky had cleared and driven the rain away.

When Tom returns, my companion moves my glass in front of me. Her long fingers hold the stem and the reflection of her ring that matches her hair wavers in the clean liquid above. The olive oscillates until its movement finally stops.

"Here's your drink," she says. "Now tell me more."

"I can't."

"Just a little. You promised to tell me how you felt."

"I did tell you."

"No you didn't. You only told me that you were sorry for what you had done. Now tell me what you really felt once you realized that your wife was pregnant."

How can I say the word?

'**N**ever show your feelings, Peter,' my mother said.

Mother, what are feelings? I know what they are! They have burst my body and touched my soul. They're more real than the world. Why shouldn't I show my feelings? They're me! The truth of me.

"**I** must know." Her head rocks against my arm. "Please, tell me."

I pull away from her and grab my glass, spilling part of my drink along the bar. "Hatred!" I say. "I hated her."

One gulp and my martini is gone. I taste only the diluted salt of the olive as I stare obstinately into my empty glass as if all answers will come once the glass is filled again.

"And what did you do?"

"I jumped from the chair I was sitting in and ran up the stairs. I was going to drag her from her bed and, if Damon was there, kill them both.

"I braced my shoulders ready to smash the door of her bedroom when suddenly I heard Gerald calling me. 'Hey, Dad. Come look at this.'

"Can you believe it? Gerald was sitting on the floor at the end of the hall with a sandwich in his hands and a glass of milk beside him looking out of the French window. My fury collapsed. As I backed away from Doreen's door, I cupped my hands together and touched them to my lips, seeing Pete's face before me instead of Doreen's.

"My body was trembling. I could hardly walk the distance from the bedroom door to the end of the hall.

"Gerald pointed at the bay and the lights of a ferry moving slowly from Manhattan to Governors Island. 'Lights on water are as fragile as the stars,' he said. 'You see them only in the dark. But if they're extinguished, all you have left is a black hole.'"

I bring the empty glass to my mouth, throw my head back and drain the one remaining drop of moisture that has collected in the depression where the olive had rested.

"I can't go on," I say. "Not tonight. Let me continue tomorrow."

"Yes," she whispers. "I'll signal to Tom. We can drink our last drink slowly."

Tom smiles at me and then takes my glass but says nothing about the olive. I'm afraid to look in the mirror.

Her hand touches my face and I feel her fingertips pressing gently on my eyelids forming shadows where nothing else exists. With fear, I brush my lips along her palm and sense the weight of her hand against my mouth.

"Keep your eyes closed," she says. "I'll tell you when Tom returns."

Only a gray eternal distance is before me.

My merry-go-round has stopped revolving and the world and I are standing still. I have no sense of movement, yet this strange immobility is my merry-go-round. I have no rings. My world is small. But I am still sitting on my wooden horse.

"You may open your eyes, now. Tom is coming."

"Here you are, Doctor. And Missus." Tom raises the glass of soda that he sips each night. "Here's to you," he says. People are calling him from along the bar but he stays with us for a minute. The three of us touch our glasses and drink.

"You know," Tom says. "When you run a place like this, you have a sense of how people feel. You know when something unpleasant might happen and you know when the crowd is having a good time, when they're happy. It's a good night tonight."

My companion and I are quiet after Tom leaves. I feel that we are alone, that we are hidden from everyone else in the bar. But I don't know what to say. We keep glancing at each other's eyes in the mirror trying not to be caught but our cunning doesn't work.

Finally she turns to me. A shy smile shows her white teeth and a hint of lipstick on her lips. "I know we've just done this. But let's do it again."

She raises her glass and I turn to her, seeing her face near mine. We touch glasses and drink.

"Don't turn away again," she says. "Look at me. Make believe you're telling me a story. A nice story."

"The only nice stories I know are old ones."

I slide her glass along the bar. "May I taste yours?" I ask.

"Whiskey after gin?"

"Just a sip." I place my mouth over the faint stain of red and let the liquid touch my lips.

"Did you like it?"

"Yes."

"May I?"

I hand my glass to her. She puts the glass to her mouth then wrinkles her nose.

We sit like two reticent kids, smiling stupidly at each other, trying desperately to think of something to say.

"As Tom said, it's a nice crowd tonight."

"Yes."

"How many people would you guess are here?"

"Oh, a hundred, maybe."

"Do you think the rain has stopped?"

"The sky was clearing a while ago."

Finally she puts her hand on mine. "For a man who works on Saturday, you'd better finish your drink and go home now." She nods to the rear of the room. "Don't forget. Walk past your friend and say something."

"I can't. I don't want to."

"I told you before that you owe it to her."

The mirror shows only a mass of faces, hiding the woman who sits alone.

"Yes," I say. "You're right." I rise from my stool longing to touch my companion beside me, longing to take her into my arms, wanting her. "Good night," is all I say.

"Good night. But don't forget. Tomorrow you're going to continue your story."

I make my way through the crowd bumping into people, squeezing past them, pardoning myself. At her table my other friend watches my approach. Could she be smiling? Impossible. She never smiles. She's only moving her red lips, moistening them with her tongue, making them glisten in the light as she always did. She adjusts the bodice of her dress then runs her fingers across her chest.

I bend over her. She smells the same as when she was young. "Good night," I say.

She lowers her eyes. "Good night. And tell her thanks."

The rain has washed the air. I take a deep breath and, with my head raised, see the forgotten moon lighting the sky. I know where I'll wait and I know what I'll wish for. I do the same thing every night until I'm bored to death with my own expectations.

Her head. Her golden hair shining in the light. Me, hurrying to reach my door before she passes. Standing like an imbecile with my back turned to the street, my forehead resting on the black painted wood listening to her steps. Knowing their sound. Waiting for what never happens. Everything draining from me.

My agonies are my dreams, the dreams of a fool. Something must happen soon before it's too late.

My heavy door closes behind me and again I'm presented with a crucial problem. What room should I sit in tonight? Surely not our bedroom. I save that pleasure until last. And why do I still call it ours? There's no such thing as ours. Ours hasn't existed in years. Not since I made everything mine.

The parlor? Why not? After all, it's the room I first knew when I entered this house as a guest of Dr. Cannon and, like a similar guest of some years later, developed a strong, if not lasting, relationship with his daughter. I had my first glass of sherry in the parlor. I struck my son in the parlor and watched his blood redden his shirt, and received the news of his death in the parlor. And it was in the parlor that I realized my wife had become pregnant by a man who could have been her son, a young man whom I admired and was grateful to.

I have kept this parlor as my sanctuary. The furniture, the mementos of forgotten people, the drapes that are copies of nineteenth century originals are my sacred objects. From the time of my eternity nothing has changed in the parlor except for the portrait of Dr. Cannon and the major events of my life that I have sacrificed at his feet. So tonight, why not make my litany here, ask my questions and answer them myself? Why not sit before the portrait of Dr. Cannon and think the few thoughts that I have left?

When it was obvious to everyone that Doreen was pregnant, Damon came to see me, not in the house, but at my office.

'Sir,' he said. 'I have moved my belongings out of your house.' He stood before my desk without the slightest remorse in his voice.

'Sit down, Damon,' I said. I was calm but all I could think of was that horrible night when I had planned to kill him and Doreen before Gerald stopped me simply by his presence in the hallway.

Damon sat in the chair that was used by patients when I took their histories. He crossed his legs. His bright eyes never left me as if it were he who was interrogating me about the approaching event of the maternity that would change our lives completely.

'Do you want me to resign my position as resident?' he asked. 'You have every right to expect it.'

I was more hesitant than he. I shifted some papers on my desk and momentarily looked away. When I looked up again, he was still staring at me.

'No.' I said. 'Not yet. I'll find something else for you.'

'Thank you, sir.'

He was about to stand, ready to leave without saying a word of what had happened.

'But Damon?' I asked. 'Why did you do it? How could you have done such a thing?'

'Sir, you should know. It wasn't I. It was you.'

He wasn't being insolent. He was just Damon, telling the truth.

'You'll always be with me, Peter,' my mother said.

When I was a young child, about the time I started school, I was frightened by the thought of death. A neighbor's dog had been run over, a dog that I was fond of. I would call to it as I passed its house and the dog would come running to me and lick my hand. Stilts was its name, a mongrel who had inherited its long legs from one of its parents.

I had heard the screech of brakes, seen a car stop and the driver get out, then watched Stilts's legs convulse in the street. The owner of the dog led me away.

'Will I die, Momma? Will I die? I don't want to die.'

My mother took me in her arms and held me close to her. 'You'll never die. You'll always be here with me.'

Now I look forward to death.

"Good night, Dr. Cannon." I bow my head at his portrait then make my way to bed, stopping only at the sideboard to replenish my supply of whiskey.

SATURDAY

It's surprising how well I feel each morning. I never remember going to sleep at night nor do I recall the last few pages of the book I was reading before my eyes closed. Yet somehow, I always manage to turn off the lights, place a bookmark at the end of a chapter, and pull the covers over my body.

But I do remember waking each morning long before dawn, looking at my watch and going to the bathroom, never being quite sure whether it was my mind or my bladder that awakened me. After that, I'm restless and must endure a long period of half-sleep during which my brain is wracked, not by my real concerns but by fictional problems that keep repeat-

147

ing themselves in my nascent consciousness.

For example, this morning, after returning to bed at 4:30 a.m. and trying to induce my weary thoughts into some sort of sleep, I found myself driving my car to the hospital down the avenue I take every day. Just after I had driven through the park and was close to my destination, a policemen in normal uniform but wearing an incredibly bright red bow tie was waving a sign that said detour, and directing traffic down a side street. As I drove down streets I didn't know, I kept thinking that I would be late for rounds. And at that instant, there I was conducting students and residents from bed to bed. No one said a word and no one attempted to examine the patients who were lying motionless beneath their white sheets with their eyes closed. We merely hesitated, looked and walked on. But, before reaching the next bed, I was miraculously transported to my car, and the same policeman with the same red bow tie was directing me down the same unknown streets while I kept thinking that I would be late for rounds.

How many times this conscious hallucination recurred I can't remember, but I was clearly aware that the frightening repetition was neither real nor a true dream. Episodes like this, in which constant imitation distorts some familiar task I do, happen to me quite frequently. The only way I can escape them is to get up at the first hint of dawn.

After I'm washed, dressed, fully awake, and have something concrete to face, I feel fine although I'm well aware that my duties of the forthcoming day could be carried out just as well, if not better, by someone else. You see, I have finally recognized the unimportance and the needlessness of my own existence. But I carry on...at least until the day is more than halfway old and my world becomes myself.

Saturday night. The bar is full of people, more crowded than ever. Heads! That's all I see. Heads—turning heads, talking heads, drinking heads, heads on pedestals, heads that float, heads hanging from invisible strings. And like my merry-go-round, the heads begin to spin, merging with the discordant sounds from a human calliope of voices until the room is nothing but a blur. Yet my mind is fixed on one image, the wooden stool that is the wooden arm that supplies me with the rings I want, the one ring I want, the ring of the golden head.

I cannot see her in the expanse of heads. I see only Tom and his weekend assistant behind the bar moving freely from customer to customer. Making my way through a wall of bodies, I distinguish only soft parts from bones, only indignant mouths from smiles.

How many times must I excuse myself?

'Never be ill-mannered, Peter,' my mother said. 'Always beg the other person's pardon. They'll think more highly of you if you do.'

And I always murmur her hollow phrase, 'Pardon me. Pardon me.' Except when I should shout it from bended knees.

At last! There she is. She's standing tonight. Must be the crowd. One elbow is on the bar and her cheek is resting against her hand. I stop my headlong struggle hoping to feast on her well-kept body, her still unbulging hips filling the contours of her dress. But through the blur of other people, only her head and her hand are visible.

"Are you going to move on, Bud?"

"Pardon me?"

"I say, are you going to move on? Or stand between my

wife and me all night?" He smiles and the woman nods.

"I beg your pardon. I'm sorry."

One step forward, the man in front of me moves to the side and I see her more fully.

Well, what's this? Usually she waits for me before she drinks. At times, half-concealed, trying to prolong the excitement of our meeting, I have watched her move her glass in circles while snatching glances in the mirror, never touching her lips until I'm next to her with my martini in my hand. But tonight her scotch is half gone. She takes another sip. I can't wait. Forget the martini. I can break rules as well as she.

I edge my way next to her and place my lips close to her ear. "You have a very fine face for a woman leaning on a bar."

She shakes her head to and fro, never taking her hand from against her cheek.

"Or should I say that I can see that at one time it was a fine face."

"Thanks a lot." She sighs and tries to smile but her face looks drawn. "Please, let's stop playing and let's not waste time tonight. I want you to continue your story right away."

"Without...."

"Without preliminaries."

"It'll be difficult."

"Because of what you have to say?"

"Yes. But also the noise. And the crowd."

Someone forces his way to the bar and pushes me in her direction. Our bodies touch and I feel her sensitive flesh against my own.

"Should we go somewhere else for a change?" I ask. "The Promenade?"

She pretends to pout. "If we did, then what would she do?"

"You mean my…wife?"

"Yes."

In the mirror I look to my other companion's habitual place but, with the heads of all the revelers blocking my vision, I can't see her table. My eyes travel the length of the room, past the long expanse of window to the door where I recognize a head of golden hair making its way slowly through the room. I know her by the way she turns and the angle at which she tilts her head, looking up now and then with innocent but inviting eyes. For a fleeting instant she sees me.

"Here you are, Doctor. Your martini. I'd been watching for you but with this crowd, I missed you."

"That's okay, Tom. You'll be busy tonight."

"I'll keep my eye on you. Just signal when you want another."

She half leans against me, her head close to mine. "Now that your…wife has seen you and you finally have your martini and your olive, you'll have to stay here."

Her breath tempts me to bring my head as close to hers as I dare, but I feel her fingers on my face gently pushing me away.

"Now that you're settled, please continue your story." Her eyes look more than worn. Her whole face looks tired. "I'm anxious to hear the end. Do you remember where you stopped last night? I do. Your wife was pregnant. And you hated her."

I let the dry flavor of gin sift slowly through the confusion that had been my mind that evening in the parlor when I realized what had been happening. Sitting before the portrait of Dr. Cannon with his benevolent eyes looking down at me, a vision of Doreen's naked body suddenly burst before me clinging desperately to another man—my resident, half her age.

151

And I heard her breath sobbing his name from the depths of her throat while I, the fool, lay in my bed just down the hall tormenting myself with guilt.

"Yes! I hated her. If she'd been next to me at that moment, I'd have strangled her."

Trying to suppress the memory, I turn my head from my companion only to catch sight of myself in the mirror. God! How horrible I look. I close my eyes to escape but, in place of my haggard face, a whole panorama of visions stampedes before my mind, beginning with my son Pete and the wound on his face and the blood on his shirt. Squeezing my lids as tightly as possible, I envison his image slowly fading and I find myself alone in an empty room staring at my hands, unable to understand.

"Hatred's like a bomb," I say, "an explosion that blows your reason to bits and tears your heart apart."

I take her hand and her fingers curl around mine. "Haven't you ever been suddenly frightened and feel that nothing can help you, especially yourself?"

"Yes. More than once."

"But, as you wait trying to recover your wits, a certain calm comes over you and your fear grows less. Hate can be like that. At first all I could think of was what Doreen had done to me. To me. You see, to me. I thought only of myself.

"But as soon as Gerald told me of the fragile lights on the bay and the black hole that might follow, I had a flood of memories about Doreen. And about what I had done. I didn't know whom to hate."

"You forgave her?"

"Not exactly. Doreen's conduct was still incomprehensible to me and I blamed her for allowing the affair to happen. But then Damon came to see me."

"He confessed?"

I laugh. "Hardly. Damon had analyzed all the events with his clear logic and told me that I was the cause of Doreen's behavior and, in turn, the cause of his."

"He did?"

"He was right of course. I understood what he meant. So I decided to ride it out. To do nothing. To see what happened."

"What did happen?"

"Nothing. Doreen carried her pregnancy with the same pride as she had with our three children. If friends or neighbors suspected anything—and I know my colleagues did after Damon left in mid-year for a residency in Manhattan—Doreen never showed it. We continued to occupy separate bedrooms but carried on our daily lives with the civility Damon had taught us."

"And how did you feel about that?"

"At first I wondered if she was laughing at my discomfort. Tormenting me for the years in which my attentions strayed. Paying me back. But then I realized Doreen wasn't like that. You see, it never dawned on me how alone she must have felt."

I laugh again and wonder why I find some things so funny. "But I know now exactly how she felt. I've had plenty of experience with being alone. Damon was right again. She needed someone to console her. And so, I tried desperately to forget the whole affair. Because…well, because I loved her still."

With her eyes closed, my companion takes her glass in both hands, throws her head back and drinks, holding the glass to her mouth long after she has swallowed. The white skin of her throat looks even whiter in the dull light and the lines of age creeping from the corners of her eyes and the edges of her lips disappear. She shifts her feet and leans more heavily on the bar.

"Let's have another," she says. "Are you ready?"

My olive stops at my lips then slides back to the bottom of the glass. I wave to Tom.

"I have a stool behind the bar, Missus," he says. "Let me bring it around for you."

"No. With all these people it'd be too much trouble."

"Not at all."

She settles on the stool and pulls her skirt to below her knees then looks at me. We're no longer close and our bodies no longer touch but her eyes are serious, their brilliant blue almost gray in the shadows of her brows. "Go on," she says. "Tell me about the child that was not yours."

'Always try to tell the truth, Peter,' my mother said. 'Because if you don't, you're almost sure to be caught.'

She had found the golden ring I had stolen from the merry-go-round hidden in the closet of my bedroom. She held the ring in front of me.

'Now, if someone at school showed you a ring like this, you might shrug your shoulders. But when I show it to you and ask you where you got it, what do you say?'

'I took it from the merry-go-round, Mom.'

She mussed my hair. 'That's what I like. The truth. Try to tell the truth. It's safer.'

"Doreen's child was born at a hospital not associated with the medical school. Not even in our neighborhood but in another district of the borough. Doreen had made all the arrangements herself without ever consulting me. I knew the obstetrician only by name.

"Late one afternoon while I was preparing to meet with my staff, I received a phone call from Gerald telling me that he was driving his mother to the hospital. I rushed there and waited in a room full of expectant fathers until a nurse congratulated me on being the father of a baby boy.

"Doreen was lying in her bed. We greeted each other only with our eyes, then she turned to the wall while I stood by the window gazing at the ice-covered limbs of the trees outside. I had an urge to rush to her side, take her hand to my lips and beg her to forgive every hurt I had ever caused her when another nurse entered with the infant and handed it to Doreen. Doreen placed the child next to her then lowered the blanket from around its face.

"I took one look. Down's Syndrome. When I was young we called them Mongolian Idiots."

In the mirror, the street outside looks the same as it always had. It hasn't changed in the forty years I've lived here. Why can't I get used to the reversed letters on the signs? Why didn't I ask someone what the Arabic scrawls meant? Would I have been less disturbed if I had? Understanding. What do I understand? Myself? Ha!

I see tears in her eyes. Fluid is collecting on the rims of her lower lids. She's biting her lip and looking up at me with an almost penitent expression, an expression that I have seen elsewhere on a face almost like hers.

"Well?" she finally asks.

"Well...."

"Please! Tell me what you felt. I must know what you felt."

"Shame. As soon as I saw that creature I felt shame. Shame that it would be associated with me. Me! The one who would be listed as the father and called the father. That's what I felt. Shame. Unforgivable, isn't it? A doctor who's supposed not only to have sympathy but to understand. And I felt shame."

She touches me but I pull away.

"But let me tell you, the shame I felt proved to be far worse than the sudden flashes of hate I have been known to express. Do you know why? Because my shame never left. It dug deeper and deeper into my soul. It was with me in every move I made. Each day I looked at the helpless thing when no one else was near and wanted to hide it so that neither others nor I could see it."

Neither of us speaks. Only the disorder of supposedly happy people surrounds us. Our eyes meet for a moment in the mirror, then we quickly look away as countless heads swirl past and I find myself on my merry-go-round, clinging to my wooden horse, trying desperately to find someone to stare at. But the contented heads I see fuse into a sea of mist as I reach in vain for rings that never come. Round and round and round I go, not knowing what is whirling, the world or me.

I pick up my glass, sip, then put it down. Again, I pick up my glass, twirl the olive, sip, then put it down. It gives me something to do. I take the glass off its cardboard coaster and place it on the wooden bar. But no ring of moisture appears. The coaster has sucked it dry. I'm afraid to finish the martini. If I do, in one fell swoop, will the olive bruise my lips or break my teeth? I take another sip and put the glass back on the coaster.

"Stop it!" she says. "Turn around and look at me. Let's end this story, once and for all."

"It's a long story. It seems that it never ends."

"It never will unless you get on with it."

I finish the martini and watch the olive settle in its bed of glass. I don't signal for Tom. I'm waiting for her.

"One evening, soon after the child was born, I was sitting in the library. Doreen was in the parlor feeding it. Breast feeding it. I tried to avoid the time of the child's feedings because...well, because each time I saw the child at breast I thought of Damon, and fantasy scenes of what must have happened between him and Doreen loomed before me larger than life. Like certain dreams, I didn't like the experience. Perhaps the scenes reminded me of myself."

My hand covers my eyes but she takes me by the wrist and moves my blinder away. "Don't do that," she whispers. "Look at me when you talk."

"Yes. I should. We promised each other, didn't we?"

She nods.

"Well, I didn't know what to do in the library so I picked up a book at random, a medical text that had long been out of print. When I was a student it had been Dr. Cannon's favorite. I was thinking of Dr. Cannon when Gerald entered without knocking and slumped to the floor in front of me.

"'Hi, Dad. What you up to?'

"'Nothing. Looking at old books. Killing time. But how did you know I was here?'

"Gerald hunched his shoulders then let them drop like rags. 'It's about that time, isn't it?'

"The expression on his face stayed the same but it dawned on me that he must have observed my recent change of habits after dinner. The library rather than the parlor. The escape from nursing time.

"'I suppose,' I said.

"'You're thinking of Grandpa, aren't you? I can tell by your face. You know, I think of Grandpa a lot too. He sure could set you thinking, couldn't he? He wanted me to be a doctor like he was and you are. He never said so but I knew.' Gerald pointed to the book I was holding. 'He used to read that book to me more than any of the others. I'll bet I can describe most of the diseases in it. But you know, Dad, being a doctor just isn't in me.'

"'What is in you, Gerald?'

"'I don't know. Guess I'm a slow starter, Dad. But I'm going to find out.'

"'Once you're in college this autumn, you'll get some ideas.'

"'You think so, Dad?'

"A week later, Doreen handed me a note. I could see that she had been crying.

Dear Mom and Dad,

I'm taking a little trip and will be gone for a long time. Don't expect to hear from me very often but don't worry. I'll be back some day.

Remember, I love you both.

Gerald

"And that was all."

Neither my companion nor I say a word. We just look at each other, our expressions as lost and incoherent as the strangers in the room, as meaningless as the desire to go round and round alone with no end in sight.

Without turning her head she reaches for her drink, our eyes remaining fixed on each other until she drains the last drop from her glass.

158

"God, it's been a long time," I say. "But I'm sure he'll keep his word. Every year Doreen and I receive separate letters. Always on our birthdays and always from a different part of the world. At least we know he's alive."

Tom walks by behind the bar and stops in front of us. "Easier on the feet, sitting. Isn't it, Missus?"

"I didn't know I was so tired," my companion says.

"You look better," Tom says as he picks up our glasses. He raises them a few inches. "No need to ask what you want, is there?"

"We're always the same, aren't we, Tom."

"It's better to stick to one thing. Be right back."

I straighten up and take a deep breath.

"You must be tired too," she says. "Standing in one spot without being able to move. Want to share the stool with me?"

"I'd love to. But then we couldn't face each other. I'd rather look at you."

"Than be next to me?"

"Not really. But I can't have both. Can I?"

She lowers her eyes and runs her fingers through her hair then takes my hand.

"What happened after your son left?" she asks.

"I'll tell you as soon as we get our drinks. Remember what I said the other night? I don't like interruptions."

"Or interludes," she whispers.

After Tom serves us, her grip tightens giving me courage to lift her hand to my lips. She makes no resistance. "Go on now," she says. "What happened?"

"For me, a nightmare. Not only worrying about Gerald...where he was, what he was doing, if he was eating right. But even more, the reasons why he left home, why he had to find out what life was about all by himself and at his age.... They were beyond my understanding. My mind was torn to pieces. I didn't know what to think.

"But worse, the child. Oh, God! The child. Looking at its slanted eyes, its open mouth, its small head. Trying to envision the physiology of its brain.

"Watching Doreen spend hours attempting to train it...and her patience with it...made my heart weep. I could only admire her. But every time I looked at the creature, I loathed it. Especially when Doreen was taking care of it.

"Of course, we had no personal life. That had finished long before. What a contrast to our first few years in the carriage house...when our lives were pure. When we thought only of each other. When love and desire were the same.

"I never had the courage to talk with Doreen about ourselves. Or was it simply myself? My needs. Lust, if you want. I was afraid she'd say no. My self-esteem had already been destroyed. But remember, I was only fifty-two when the child was born."

"And your wife? How old was she?"

"Forty-five."

"How do you think she felt?"

"I don't know.... I'd never thought about it."

Her hand is still in mine. Again I raise it, not to my lips but only to see it, to look at it, to make certain that it's still there.

"You've heard me often enough," I whisper. "You know my problem. Thinking only of myself."

"Maybe that's everyone's problem. Whether we desire or we give."

We say nothing for a while. My eyes wander to the mirror

but I ignore the sea of heads, searching instead for the table in the rear. Do I see her hair hidden in the comfort of the crowd? I can't tell. I see only the street, penetrating first through the mirror and then through the pane of glass, showing me the things I cannot understand.

"What are you waiting for?" she asks. "I want you to finish. I want to hear how the story ends."

"Yes. You're right. We must finish."

Her eyes are lowered, looking at our hands cupped together as if we were walking along a darkened street, grasping the only thing we dared to know.

"We had a pleasant break, an intermission in our lives…lives that had grown more stiff and artificial with time…when Reen came back home to attend medical school. I'd had high hopes that things would change once someone from the family was with us again. And they did. Or at least they seemed to when the three of us were together. But it didn't last for long. At Christmas, Reen asked me if she could move into the carriage house. Of course, I said yes.

"With that done, Doreen and I more or less returned to our former habits although the tension between us seemed more relaxed. Nothing much…but a shaky easiness crept into the routine of our lives. We talked to each other more normally than we had, not about anything important but about the happenings around the house. Perhaps we were merely adapting to each other.

"Still, that damn child was there. Just the thought of it repelled me.

"In the evenings when I was home, Doreen liked to tell me of the child's progress.

"'Guess what Baby did today?'

"*Baby! Baby!* So unlike Doreen. It was worse than *Junior*.

"'He ate cookies all by himself and said, "More. More. More."'

"I smiled politely while pleading to myself, Why? Why? Why? All this wasted effort. That genetic blunder can develop only so far and then stop.

"'This Sunday you must listen to the words he knows.'

"The words he knows. His fumbling attempts to speak with his large tongue and his dribbling nose. I hated them.

"Oh, I knew what was the matter, although I couldn't admit it to myself. The child had taken my place. I was jealous of all the attention Doreen gave to it."

"And your wife? What did she think?"

"I don't know what she thought."

"Why didn't you know what she thought? You'd been married to the woman for...how many years?"

"Twenty-six."

"And you didn't know her?"

"Sometimes I thought she was playing the role of martyr. Making up for her own...what do you call them nowadays... sins, indiscretions? If only I had had the courage to talk to Doreen and convince her to place the child in a home for the mentally retarded, would we have had a chance? I felt sure that we would.

"But I was wrong. Time itself finally answered me. No. Not a chance in a million. Because after the child died, my hopes of a reconciliation never materialized."

My companion tilts her head and moves closer to me, the thin lines around her eyes deepening as she frowns. With each breath she takes, I watch her breasts rise and fall until her hand touches her chest and her fingers grip into her smooth skin.

"Why didn't you talk to her? Tell her how you felt? What you wanted?"

"How could I? I was more fearful than ever."

"Of what?"

"Of what she knew."

She backs away and whispers, "You were afraid of what she knew?"

"Yes. It was Doreen's calmness, her impassive acceptance of the death of the child that worried me most. I couldn't believe it. She became...what shall I say... detached? I'd catch her looking at me...sometimes as if she didn't know me and other times as if her heart were overflowing with sympathy."

I lift my glass to my mouth. The martini is lukewarm. And it's already my third. I can't rush my drink because the supply is limited and I have almost reached the end. I merely wet my lips. The olive slips towards me then hesitates as if floating.

"Whenever I saw a hint of tenderness in her eyes, I began to hope. But nothing intimate ever pursued. Not a word. Not a gesture. Not an action.

"And then, several months after the child died, another hope was destroyed, making my life even more depressing than it was. Reen told us that she had accepted an internship in Seattle. Can you imagine? Seattle. Three thousand miles away. The other side of the continent. Just one more disappointment to add to my list."

I laugh, but the thought of what happened after that is breaking my heart.

"What are you laughing about now?"

"Just thinking about the old married couple being alone at last. Just the two of us. Like our first year of marriage. Alone in the carriage house."

"Your sense of humor can be…."

"I know. Don't tell me. It wasn't funny. It pains me more than anyone. Oh, God! How different those two periods of our lives were."

I look at my drink and slide it towards me. I would love to taste it, tepid or not. I would love to roll the olive with my tongue then bite it, pretending it was the first of many. But I still have a long way to go in my story, the time condensed into monotony but the agony stretched as far as my arms can reach.

"'Peter,' Doreen said one evening. We were sitting in the parlor reading. Doreen was on a couch and I in Dr. Cannon's favorite chair. 'Now that Reen has left, do you mind if I move into the carriage house?'

"I said nothing. I didn't know what to say. How do you explain feelings? They get so mixed up. Like thoughts. You see, despite what had happened…what she had done. And all the things that I had done…if nothing else, I wanted to be near her. I loved her. And I wanted her to love me again. I guess I was living under the delusion that if love had ever been real, a hidden curative effect must lie somewhere in its depths.

"'What did you say?' I asked.

"'Do you mind if I move into the carriage house?'

"'Why do you want to do that, Doreen?'

"'I don't know. But sometimes I get this foreboding that something is about to happen.'

"'What?'

"'When we're together, I feel afraid.'

"'Afraid? Of me?'

"'No.' She looked away for a moment.'Not ·physically afraid.' Then she laughed, almost like she used to. 'And not specifically of you. A strange sensation comes over me. I don't think that I can explain it.'

"'Try.'

"'I want to say that it's a feeling as if I'm falling. As if my breath is being sucked out of me. But it's not. It's as if everyone I have ever known...and I can't even recognize them...were rushing past me and I was struggling to hold them where they belonged.'

"'And you feel like this when you're with me?'

"'Only when I'm alone with.you. Stupid, isn't it?'

"'Tell me. Was it what I've done?'

"'No one does things by himself, Peter. Whatever was done, was done by both of us. And regret keeps consuming our lives. It's when we're together that I feel the most anguish.'

"'I understand but....'

"She stood up. I thought for a moment that she was reaching for me, that she would pull me to her as she had pulled me to my feet that first night we had met. But instead, she backed away.

"'Let me try the carriage house for a while, Peter.' She smiled as she walked towards the door. 'I don't think I could be completely without you. We'll see each other. We'll keep up appearances...at school functions and things like that. Okay? That wouldn't be dishonest, would it?'

"'In other words, we'll be friends,' I said.

"'Yes.'

"We kept our separation as quiet as possible. Of course, it wasn't long before our neighbors and all my colleagues knew."

The courage to grab my companion overcomes my caution. I seize her by the shoulders, drawing her as close to me as our separate positions allow. "What do you think about a set-up like that?"

"Please." She closes her eyes and turns her head away. "Don't ask me."

"Do you want to know what I think?"

She nods. I see only her cheek, the contour of her nose, her quivering chin. "Yes," she whispers.

"A mockery! A sham! That's what it was. Friends! As if marriage was manners. As if something personal was manners. Marriage is tender and savage at the same time. Only two people know what their life together is like. What their feelings are. What they want from the other. Their dreams. Their thoughts. At times the unreality of the other. It's taking from one and giving to the other, a physical collision that smashes one into the other in the ultimate joy of knowing each other."

She opens her eyes and looks at me. "And why didn't you tell her that, too?"

I close my eyes and long for my merry-go-round. Oh, how desperately I long for my merry-go-round.

"Because I'm a coward."

Gradually I release my hold on her shoulders. My fingers feel cold away from the thin cloth covering her skin, but she takes my hands in hers and presses them against her thigh.

"One Sunday afternoon in June we met by chance on the Promenade. Oh, we had met any number of times before, at social occasions or on the street where we would exchange a few words but, except for the shallow chatter of the moment, we had never talked.

"The Promenade was crowded. Kids were chasing each other, making hazards of themselves on bicycles while young couples, oblivious of others, were petting and kissing, heedless of what they did. We walked away from a group of teenagers dancing to the blare of a radio until we saw an empty place, barely big enough for two, at the very end of one of the long benches overlooking the river.

"'Do you want to sit down for a while?' I asked.

"'Yes. If we can fit,' she laughed.

"Next to us was an old couple half asleep in the sun with handkerchiefs covering their eyes. Every once in a while a gurgling snore came from the man's throat.

"'You used to snore like that,' she said.

"'I did not.'

"'How do you know?'

"'I don't. But if you say so, I believe you.'

"We really didn't say much to each other. It was as if we had forgotten how to talk. But the feeling that our being together stirred in my heart was like the first realization of life to a child, of not knowing, or caring, but only wanting. I wanted to sit on the bench forever. I wanted her voice to say whatever it wished. I wanted to turn and look at her. But I was afraid. In that crowd of people, the noise, the motion, the snoring, I was afraid to turn my head."

'Never show your fear, Peter,' my mother said. 'If you do, others will take advantage of you. Always act brave. Get the upper hand.' Dear Mom. Dear Mother. Can we ever change ourselves? Or do we simply hide behind what we have been taught, feigning what we know will work?

"Finally, I looked at her, not full on but with my head bent so that I could barely see her face.

"She had one eye closed and was pointing with her finger, drawing a long rectangle in the air.

"'When you're sitting on a bench, the fence interferes with your view, doesn't it?' she asked. 'It cuts the wharves just below us and the skyscrapers across the river into long framed compartments. As if the tops of the buildings had been chopped off and only the sky itself were free.'

"I looked straight ahead at one of the new glass towers of Manhattan and, through two black fence posts, saw only part of the building. As my eye traveled along the river to the old fish market, the compartments became progressively smaller and I saw progressively less.

"'Sort of like us,' I said. 'We all live in separate compartments.'

"'Shall we smash them?' she asked.

"'How?'

"'By standing up and looking over the fence.'

"We put our elbows between the spikes of the railing and leaned as far forward as we could. I felt as if we had left the world behind and were looking at the silent skyline for the first time.

"'That's better,' she said. 'Now we can see more.' She pointed to her left. 'Look. There goes the ferry to Staten Island. Remember all the boats we used to watch at night? The thousands of lights twinkling on the water?' And then she laughed. 'Come on, walk me home. You know where I live.'

"Walking down our shaded street, still smelling of spring trees and cut grass, I headed for the carriage house. But half a block before we reached it, she stopped in front of her father's house, the house in which I live.

"'Don't come any further,' she said. 'I'm glad we met, Peter. I've missed talking to you.'

"'Then…why don't we meet more often?'

"She looked one way and then the other. The street was empty. She laughed. 'It's hard to stop what you're used to, isn't it? The habits you create in a lifetime are like drugs. I guess we become addicted to what we know.'

"'How about once a week?' I asked. 'We'll meet on the Promenade and talk. Not on Sunday when it's crowded but…would Friday evening do? We wouldn't exactly be alone, you know. There's always someone on the Promenade.'

"She bowed her head. 'Okay. Every Friday evening we'll meet and talk. But no more than talk.'

"She started to walk away but then turned. 'Why don't we meet at the bar instead?' she said. 'The bar you took me to the night we met. And let's make a game of it. Let's make believe we meet by accident, like we did that first time near the Penny Bridge.'

"And that's how our meetings began."

My companion is rubbing the back of my hand, pressing the tips of my fingers gently against her thigh when she reaches for her drink. She looks at the glass before she attempts to lift it as if she were analyzing the color. The level of the liquid wavers against the rim but she lowers her head to it and takes a sip. Then she looks at me.

"Is that the end of your story?"

"I don't know."

"You forgot one part."

"What's that?"

"You didn't tell me how your wife's last child died."

My martini is now warm, almost as warm as my hand that holds it. I taste the earthy flavor of vermouth more than I like. Has the alcohol evaporated, leaving more of the residue? I would hate to add ice.

"May I tell you tomorrow?"

Her hand is again on mine, transmitting its weight through mine onto her lap. Only her dress and her white slip separates us.

"Yes. If you wish, tell me tomorrow."

Again she raises her glass to her lips and looks at it, not as she did before but with surprise. "Look," she says. "We've hardly touched our last drinks. So you must tell me a little more. Now, what can you tell me? I know. Tell me again how you first met your wife. I've forgotten parts of it."

"The beginning?"

"Yes. The beginning."

"Well, I was a young medical student living a few blocks from the old medical school, a simple and lonely medical student who liked to walk by myself in the evenings through a neighborhood I thought was luxurious. And my favorite spot was the bluff above the river, green and lush and quiet, giving a view of Manhattan that only sea gulls could have known. At sunset, the sky glowed in the west like a fire where the colors of day gradually merged with those of night.

"One spring evening, an evening that smelled of blossoms and was as warm as summer, I was sitting on the ground not far from the Penny Bridge. Before me, the silhouettes of the tall buildings of Manhattan looked like church steeples in the setting sun and the ships plodding the river and the bay were like toys waiting for Christmas.

"Two bare legs stopped in front of me. All I saw were a

pair of saddle shoes, anklets, and threads of golden hair sprouting from shapeless stems.

"A gruff voice said, 'What are you doing sitting there?'

"And then I saw her knees, as plump and unexciting as a child's. But before I knew what was happening she squatted in front of me, took my hand, and pulled me to my feet. I fell against her, holding her shoulders for an instant, but saw only her golden hair. Without knowing what she really looked like, I felt something change inside me right then and there.

"She asked me to walk with her. The trees were full and the light that filtered from the street lamps fell in patches, disguising her face in shadows. To hide my fear I asked her if she'd like a drink, so we came to this bar...the bar we're in now...and when I saw her in the light for the first time, I knew that I was in love."

She leans her brow against my shoulder then raises her glass, her eyes fresher than they have been all night. "Thank you," she says. "Come. Touch your glass to mine. We'll drink what's left in one fell swoop like a toast...as if we were celebrating."

"To us," each of us whispers as we throw our heads back and drink.

She smiles and points to my olive. "You forgot your favorite part."

"No, I didn't."

"What are you saving it for?"

"For us."

Tilting the glass, I retrieve the olive with my fingers and point the pimento at her. "Half for you. And half for me."

She opens her mouth and her white teeth bite the olive in two, her lips touching my fingers. I bring the remains to my own mouth allowing my lips to touch where hers have been.

"Will you walk with me along the Promenade tonight?" I ask. "I know every building on Manhattan and every light that shines on the water."

Barely tilting her head, she appeals to me with her eyes. "Not tonight. Really, I'd like to. But I'm a little tired. But I promise that tomorrow night I'll walk with you for sure."

Her eyes motion towards the back of the room. "But before you go, say goodnight to your friend at her table."

"Why must you always think of her?"

She shrugs her shoulders. "Forgetting someone is the worst thing we can do. And recognizing them is the least."

I kiss her forehead then walk away through the crowd.

My head is as light as a merry-go-round. Other heads in the room no longer exist. They have disappeared. They have floated away or melted into the sweet-smelling air. I see only bodies that respond to my command of 'Pardon me.' My wooden horse moves up or down or sideways, I know not what, until the last obstacles separate and I see her, my lady of the night.

Dwarfed by those around her, the small surface of her table is empty except for her glass and her hand. She raises the glass to the level of my face, throws her head back and swallows.

Her eyes flash at me. "Thank you for coming." More true to form, she looks away and speaks in her heavy whisper. "You're told to say good night, aren't you?"

"Yes."

"Do you really want to?"

As I drift away again on my merry-go-round, more soberly this time, I count my metal rings. Each ring is a treasure in itself and a thrill to hold, but only one is gold. I stole a gold ring once, still hidden in the drawer of my desk. My mother knew about it. No one else. I couldn't lie to my mother.

"Yes. I do."

"But you never had a real choice, did you?" she asks.

"I'm sorry." I place my head close to hers. "Good night," I whisper.

It's later tonight than usual and darkness hangs over the street making the street lamps glow more brightly on objects close to them. From the shadows I see a vague, luminous spot moving along the sidewalk. Gradually the spot takes form. Below it, a body holds it upright. Legs carry it along. Igniting into gold, like a flame before it's extinguished, a sunset before it sinks, its color dulls the light from the lamp.

I rush ahead to my door and hug its polished wood, camouflaging my hunger with sound. Footsteps that begin as hope reach their crescendo then fade into tomorrow.

Tonight I choose the parlor again. I need to look at Dr. Cannon. I need all the strength that I can get. At the windows, his brocade drapes are drawn. His sherry decanter is on the table. His chair that I'm sitting in is comfortable. I have positioned it to face him, just far enough away from his portrait to avoid extending my neck.

Help me, Dr. Cannon.

Five years of humiliation. That's what I had. Five years! Why? The thing wasn't even mine. But it had my name and it lived in my house and I had to look at its small head and flat face every day. Five years and still sleeping in a crib at night. Five years and talking in disconnected phrases. Breathing through its mouth like an old lady ready to die. Dribbling.

Hopeless! There was nothing that could be done for it. Five years and my wife paid more attention to it than she did to me.

I remember that evening distinctly. The evening when the thought of what to do first struck me.

I had just returned from attending the monthly staff meeting. It was late. Doreen was standing at the parlor door. I can see her now, the tired look on her face. Her sweater was draped over the chair I'm sitting in at this very moment

'Good evening, Peter,' she said. 'I've been waiting for you. Baby has a cold and I'm rather worried about him.'

'Not another?'

'Yes. It started a couple of days ago but seems to be getting worse. He hasn't eaten all day. I can't even get him to drink water. I think you ought to look at him.'

I examined him, much against my will. His breathing was heavy and he was coughing. I remember touching his skin. I hated to touch him. He was hot. I took his temperature. 102.4. A few rales in his right lower lung hardly surprised me.

'We'd better give him antibiotics,' I said. 'Just as a precaution.' I turned to her. 'Would you get my bag in the hall closet, please?'

I looked at the child struggling in its crib. And suddenly...That's when it dawned on me. Bang! Just like that.

And then the thought grew. To have an empty crib. No crib at all. A bedroom where eventually we might be together again. Yes. All we needed was a little time. Wounds heal. Sometimes you can't even find the scars.

I injected the child with sterile water.

The last dose I gave three days later is even more vivid in my memory than the first. The child's eyes were sunken. He was struggling for breath. His head heaved as he sucked air into his open mouth. His lips were dry.

'Do you think we should take him to the hospital?' Doreen asked.

'We'll see in the morning.'

I put the empty ampoule in my pocket as I had done with the others. Doreen looked straight at me for what seemed an eternity, a strange glimmer in her eyes. And then she looked at the child.

At 4:00 a.m. next morning she woke me. The child was dead.

"Dr. Cannon? What should I tell her tomorrow?"

'Always *try to tell the truth, Peter,' my mother said. 'Because if you don't, you're almost sure to be caught.'*

How many times did she tell me that?

One last look at Dr. Cannon. But I turn my head away. The blue of his eyes is too bright for the time of night. I switch off the lights to the parlor and leave it in darkness. The thick carpet of my stairway silences my footsteps. I close my bedroom door and am alone again in the night. Tomorrow. Tomorrow evening. Yes. My gift for tomorrow. And I must hurry tomorrow along because time has been slipping from me like suds from dirty hands.

My bottle. But just a taste to put me in the mood for sleep. And perhaps my radio rather than a book tonight.

I hear an old song. From how many years ago?

SUNDAY

Today is the day I dislike most. What can I do on Sunday? Going to the hospital to pretend that I'm working in my office is out of the question. I don't have that much to do anymore. Before I gave up private practice, at least my Sunday mornings were occupied by rounds and, during the rest of the day, an occasional emergency call might break the monotony.

Yet, out of habit, I leave the house as early on Sunday as on any other day of the week, get my car and drive to a few of my favorite spots not far from home. The streets are empty, almost ghostly, on this day of rest making it easier to reach my random choice of the morning, be it poor old Coney Island or the lonely flats of Jamaica Bay. But once there, as if in retaliation for breaking the strictures of the day, I find myself with more time on my hands than I know what to do with.

More often than not I drive through Prospect Park. It's close and in the early morning it's always pleasant, whether in spring when the rhododendrons are in bloom or in winter with snow blanketing the meadow. I drive on the same roads over and over again as if on a never-ending treadmill and see the same scenes repeatedly but, no matter how much I'm tempted, I hesitate to walk the lanes of the park at such a lonely hour.

After I have exhausted as much of the early morning as I can, I return home, park my car for the day, then walk through the neighborhood from church to church just to watch the parishioners coming from their different services.

Then lunch. I've always hated to eat alone, especially in a restaurant, or even worse, to make the effort of cooking for myself. On rare Sundays the Lebanese and Syrian restaurants tempt me, but if I succumb, instead of enjoying a food I love, I'm beset with memories. More often than not, I simply settle for a sandwich at home or a bowl of canned soup.

Once my Sunday drive is accomplished and lunch finished I'm at a complete loss. How to spend the afternoon? I never know what to do but usually end up with one of the same three choices: reading *The Times*, reading a medical journal, or walking along the Promenade. Pacing back and forth along the Promenade is more like it.

But today, the Promenade is out. Today is special, the most special day I've had in years. I shall save the pleasure of the Promenade for the evening when the one I need will walk with me. Oh how I've longed to be with her on the Promenade in the evening after the crowds have thinned, after the light has faded from the sky. I'll take her arm in mine or, better still, place my arm around her waist. My hand will feel the rhythm of her body as she walks and my fingertips will sense the pulsing of the heart I love. Tonight, Manhattan will glow more brightly than ever before and the clusters of light plying the river and the bay will dance with joy.

Should I propose a restaurant?

I'm early. At least half an hour early. But I couldn't stand sitting with *The Times* for another minute. Can you imagine reading *The Times*, *The Sunday Times*, all afternoon and never finishing? Dropping the different sections on the floor and trying to find them again? And at the same time worrying what I should tell her about the death of the child. Oh, God! When she hears, will she burst my dream? Will I be worse off than I was? Could she already know? Is she just waiting to hear the truth pour from my heart?

That's why I'm early. I just had to see someone, anyone, to grow accustomed to people before I saw her. I must move my lips, talk again and try to calm myself. Then, when I'm perfectly composed, I'll walk up to her, forget my usual lines and simply tell her. I promised that I would. And I'll tell her the truth. I'll be honest. My mother warned me about honesty.

As I open the door, the air of the empty bar hits me like a cold draft. The few familiar standbys are tossing comments back and forth from widely separated stools while the old man who comes only on Sunday evening sits by himself near the door, talking to no one but sifting through a handful of worn post cards.

"Hi, Tom."

"Good evening, Doctor. A little early tonight."

"Yes. I had nothing else to do so...."

"I'm sure you want to wait."

"Yes."

"Then how about a glass of soda with a piece of lemon?"

"Okay."

"I drink it all night long myself. Keeps my lips wet and my customers think I'm drinking with them."

"We all have tricks, don't we, Tom?"

"Not really a trick, Doctor. People like to think you're part of them. That you understand them."

"That's hard to do sometimes."

"Depends on what they've done and who's listening."

"What do you think's more important, Tom?"

"Who's listening."

I can't keep my eyes from her empty stool. It's so neat, so still, so properly aligned against the uncluttered bar. As clean as a newly made hospital bed after the turbulence of death, awaiting the innocence of another occupant.

Just last night, with the hoard of people crowding us, pushing, squeezing us, we kept touching inadvertently. Is that why I had the courage to kiss her forehead? But she didn't object. She didn't back away.

Soon, as soon as she comes, with no one near us, when I'm sitting next to her with only our own two glasses on the bar, when we can whisper instead of shout, the first thing I'll say is, 'Forgive me for what I'm about to tell you. Because I can never forgive myself.' And then I'll tell her what I did. And I'll wait.

What will she do? Will she walk away? Destroy my hopes?

But hasn't she already forgiven me for my selfishness...my anger...my loss of control? She's listened to me confess these faults and has touched me, taken my hand to her knee, leaned her forehead against my shoulder as if she understood. Each time I leave she tells me to say good night to...my wife.

But, damn it, where is she? She should have been here by now. She couldn't have walked along the Promenade by herself as she did a few evenings ago. She has no reason to. Besides, we're walking along the Promenade tonight. The both of us. Together. Yes. Just the two of us after the sun has set. We'll stop at a quiet spot with no one near us. We'll lean over the railing and look across the river and the bay. We'll talk about lights and water, the beauty of the view...and things of more importance.

"Tom!"

He hurries towards me. "Yes, Doctor. Want something?"

"The time. I think my watch is wrong."

His watch shows the same time as mine.

"I wouldn't worry, Doctor. She's never failed you, has she?"

"No, not really.... Maybe once or twice."

"That makes a Grade A student, Doctor. You should know that."

"Yes. I do."

Tom's glance shifts from me towards the door. Almost imperceptibly his mood changes. In the mirror, I see my other friend. She's holding the door partly open, her eyelids closed and her head downcast. Suddenly, for a mere second, our eyes meet in the mirror and she slams the door.

Without looking at me again she walks slowly through the room, her head high and her hips swaying as they always have. Passing the empty tables, she reaches the small table with one chair, sits and stares at me.

Tom has already poured her whiskey.

"Excuse me, Doctor."

Like a teacher questioning an errant student, she looks at me, her eyes piercing me as they have never done before.

Stop. Don't look at me that way. You're supposed to hide what you believe.

Finally she takes a drink then puts her hand to her forehead, relieving me of trying to resolve her thoughts. During all those years I never really knew what went through her mind. She only tried to please me. Only gave. I've often wondered if regret has scarred her life, if the sequel to her expectations has proved the same as mine.

Yet, whenever I'm near her, an unnerving sense of relief overtakes me, a dependence that buoys my failing strength. And I think to myself, what would I do if she wasn't here? It has always been like that. You see, I need. And I know I need. I needed my mother. My father. Dr. Cannon. My wife. My...friend. Especially my merry-go-round.

But tonight my merry-go-round will be still and without a sound. Because now, I need only the one that I am waiting for.

Look! What do you think of that? From her table in the rear, she's beckoning to me. Again! Her hand is calling me. She's never done that before.

Moving only my eyes, I look in all directions. Tom is talking to two of his customers while the old man near the door is holding a post card close to his face and is laughing.

It's my turn now to walk past the empty tables but my eyes remain on the stool next to the bar where my companion should be sitting. I don't like the quiet or the expanded dimensions of the room tonight.

"Sit down," she says. I put my soda next to her glass, turn, and take a chair from another table.

"Put the chair there." She points to the spot opposite her which places my back to the bar and blocks my view.

She leans forward. Her dresses always were too low. Especially now that she has aged.

"What are you doing here?" she asks. "Why don't you go find her?"

"What do you mean?"

"You don't know? You call yourself a doctor? And you fail to see what even I can see?"

She points in the direction of the bar. "No. Don't turn. No one's there."

"But she's supposed to...."

"Don't you realize that she's sick? You sit on the stool next to her and look at her all night long. Haven't you seen her take pills? Hold her chest? I can see the pain on her face from here. I've even jotted down the number of times you've missed it."

"What are you talking about?"

"Your wife is sick. Go to her."

My glass touches my lips but instead of the clean smack of gin, bubbles fill my mouth, breaking against my membranes like sparklers in the night. In my glass the small morsel of fruit floats instead of sinks and is yellow instead of green.

She leans towards me again. Thousands of lines converge at the cleft between her breasts.

"Do you want me to go with you?" she asks. "You may not know it, but we have become acquaintances."

Her eyes are the same blue as they were and her lips the same red.

"No. No, I think it would be better...."

"I understand.... But get going."

The long rays of sun are hot but my stomach is shuddering with cold. The street lamp near where I wait for her to pass stands useless in the daylight but the trees along our street protect me as I rush along. My pace slows before our house where a spot of sun, escaping through the leaves, hits the brass foot plates of our entrance doors.

I'm running now. Gasping. My breath is short. I can hardly breathe but I reach the carriage house where purple irises are in bloom along the patch of earth leading to the door.

The bell is sounding in the hallway. I press again. And again and again. Wait.

I have a key.

"Doreen!"

The hallway next to the old stable is long and is painted white. Small watercolors and photos of the Heights, old ones and new ones, decorate the walls.

"Doreen!"

A crazy house. Fun. First, at the end of the hall, is the bedroom. Then the stairway to upstairs, then the kitchen and finally the long and narrow living room on the other side of the stable.

"Doreen!"

The bedroom door is open. Her golden hair. That's all I see. She's sitting in her chair facing the rear window to the garden and next to her is a table. My photo. When I was a resident.... But her reading light is on.

"Doreen. It's Peter."

Her hand is cold. No pulse. Her eyes....